# DREAMWORKS

# MADAGASCAR 3

## THE NOVEL

D0951332

PRICE STERN SLOAN
An Imprint of Penguin Group (USA) Inc.

PRICE STERN SLOAN
Published by the Penguin Group
Penguin Group (USA) Inc., 375 Hudson Street,
New York, New York 10014, USA
Penguin Group (Canada), 90 Eglinton Avenue East, Suite 700,
Toronto, Ontario M4P 2Y3, Canada
(a division of Pearson Penguin Canada Inc.)
Penguin Books Ltd., 80 Strand, London WC2R 0RL, England
Penguin Group Ireland, 25 St. Stephen's Green, Dublin 2, Ireland
(a division of Penguin Books Ltd.)
Penguin Group (Australia), 250 Camberwell Road,
Camberwell, Victoria 3124, Australia
(a division of Pearson Australia Group Pty. Ltd.)
Penguin Books India Pvt. Ltd., 11 Community Centre,
Panchsheel Park, New Delhi—110 017, India
Penguin Group (NZ), 67 Apollo Drive, Rosedale, Auckland 0632, New Zealand
(a division of Pearson New Zealand Ltd.)
Penguin Books (South Africa) (Pty.) Ltd., 24 Sturdee Avenue,
Rosebank, Johannesburg 2196, South Africa

Penguin Books Ltd., Registered Offices: 80 Strand,
London WC2R 0RL, England

Madagascar 3 © 2012 DreamWorks Animation L.L.C. Published by
Price Stern Sloan, a division of Penguin Young Readers Group,
345 Hudson Street, New York, New York 10014. *PSS!* is a registered
trademark of Penguin Group (USA) Inc. Printed in the U.S.A.

ISBN 978-0-8431-6903-4                    10 9 8 7 6 5 4 3 2 1

It was a beautiful day on the plains of Africa. The sun was shining and the birds were singing. And the hum of a plane's engine could be heard.

"Music!" Skipper ordered the other Penguins. "Thrusts?"

"Check!" Rico shouted.

"Flaps?" Skipper asked.

"Check!" Kowalski reported.

"Diamonds and gold?" Skipper wanted to know.

"Check!" Kowalski said.

The Penguins piled into their monkey-powered Super-Plane and took off.

On the ground, a group of animals—Alex the lion,

Marty the zebra, Melman the giraffe, and Gloria the hippo—who used to live in the New York Zoo, called out to the plane.

"Bye! We're going to miss you! Have a safe flight. Don't forget about us!" the Zoosters said.

"We'll be back from Monte Carlo in a couple of weeks," Skipper called down to them. "Or whenever the gold runs out." The Penguins planned to gamble their gold away at the casinos in Monte Carlo.

"All right! We'll be waiting for you!" Alex said.

"Just kidding!" Skipper told them. "We're never coming back!"

"What?!" Alex cried out in disbelief.

"Private! Initiate warp drive!" Skipper shouted.

The plane went into warp drive and disappeared. Alex was stunned.

"Did they just say they are never coming back?" Alex asked. He looked around. His friends were gone. "Guys? Marty? Melman? Gloria?"

"Help! Help! Alex! I'm over here!" Alex heard Marty call.

Alex raced over to a hunched-over Marty.

"What is it, Marty? I'm here!"

"Oh, goody. Here, chew on this, will ya?" Marty wanted Alex to chew his food for him! What was going on? This wasn't Marty; this was an *old* Marty. An old Marty without teeth!

Alex screamed, stepped back, and tripped over a log.

Actually, it wasn't a log; it was Melman's leg!

"What is going on? Why are you so old and covered in liver spots?"

But Melman didn't answer. He was fast asleep. And snoring!

Just then, Gloria spoke up. "Look who's talking!"

Gloria was old, too. "When was the last time you looked in a mirror?" she asked Alex.

"What?" Alex asked.

"Gotta go," Gloria said. "Got me the time warp drive!" And with that, Gloria disappeared, just like the Penguins' plane.

Alex still couldn't figure out what was going on. Then he saw a mirror and decided to check himself out.

*"Ahhhh!"* He screamed in horror. Alex was old, too!

The next thing he knew, someone was shaking him. "Wake up, Ally-Al! Wake up!"

Alex rubbed his eyes. "Marty?" he asked. Yes, it was Marty—the *real* Marty. It was all a dream, a terrible dream, a nightmare!

"I'm glad you're up," Marty told him, "'cause I got a surprise for you."

"What is it? Is it the Penguins?" Alex asked excitedly. Even though Alex had dreamed that the Penguins took off, they really had—that part of Alex's nightmare was true. The Penguins really went to Monte Carlo, and the Zoosters were stuck in Africa.

"Nope. But it's the next best thing," Marty told him.

Marty put his hooves over Alex's eyes and led him up a hill.

"Okay, watch out, watch yourself," Marty warned as Alex stumbled over some rocks. "Sorry, little incline there," Marty apologized after Alex nearly fell. "Back up this hill, and . . . "

*Whack!* Alex hit his head on a branch.

4

"Watch out, low-hanging branch," Marty warned, a little too late. "Just over this bluff and *voilà*!" Marty removed his hooves from his friend's eyes.

Disoriented, Alex tumbled down the hill!

*"Ahh!"* Alex screamed as he rolled head over foot. As he came to a stop, he heard Marty announce, "Happy birthday, pal!"

Alex looked up and couldn't believe what he saw. "Wow, New York City!" he shouted.

Alex rubbed his eyes. Could that really be New York City? The very place where his beloved New York Zoo was? But he was in Africa, not in New York; what was going on?

As he looked more closely, he saw that it wasn't really New York City; it was just a model, made of dirt and mud. Gloria was dressed as the Statue of Liberty, and Melman's neck was a bridge that spanned from Long Island to Manhattan.

"Surprise!" Gloria and Melman shouted.

Alex was touched that his friends had done all that for him. "Gloria, you're Lady Liberty, and Melman, you're the Brooklyn Bridge," Alex observed.

"You got it," Gloria said with a smile.

But Melman looked disappointed. "Actually, I'm the Triborough Bridge."

"Wow! You guys made this?" Alex asked his friends, ignoring Melman's correction.

"Yep. From memory!" Marty told him. "From crazy, obsessive memory!"

Like a little kid, Alex ran right into the middle of the model. "Hey, Fifth Avenue with no traffic!" he shouted with glee.

Marty, Gloria, and Melman beamed, glad that their friend liked what they had created.

"There's Times Square, with its modern-day corporate lack of character," Alex continued. "And the Chrysler Building! And the zoo!"

Alex paused over the lifelike mud zoo and studied the miniature versions of himself and his friends in their enclosures.

"Wow! Our home. Look, there's a little me. And little all of us-es."

Alex closed his eyes and remembered his glory days at the zoo, when he was the king—the star attraction. He pictured himself up on that rock, striking his pose and roaring. The crowd went wild, and his heart soared with pride. And behind him were his biggest fans—his pals Marty, Gloria, and Melman holding ALEX IS #1 foam fingers. The four friends laughed and laughed. Yes, those were the days.

Suddenly, Alex snapped back to reality. He wasn't in the zoo. He wasn't even in New York City. He was here, in Africa. Tears filled his eyes, and he started to bawl. He looked at his friends, who were crying, too.

"You guys have both made and ruined my day," Alex said, blowing his nose.

Trying to lighten the mood, Gloria pulled out Alex's birthday cake. "Make a wish," she told the lion.

Alex shut his eyes, his tears nearly dousing all the candles. He drew in a deep breath and blew out the remaining candles, just as the Lemurs—Julien, Mort, and Maurice—popped out of the cake.

"Ta-da! Your wish has come true!" Julien, king

of the Lemurs, shouted as cake and icing sprayed everywhere.

"Oh yay! My tummy is speaking to me," Mort said with a mouthful of cake. And then he threw up!

"Gross!" Gloria, Melman, Marty, and Alex shouted.

"I wouldn't eat that side of the cake if I were you," Julien commented. "Mort's vomit is not very delicious. I know. I've tried it."

And with that, Gloria picked up the cake and the Lemurs and tossed them aside.

"What was your wish?" Gloria asked Alex.

"I wished we could go home," Alex told her. "I mean, don't get me wrong, I love this, but it's not the real thing," he said, pointing to the New York City model.

"Well, that's because it's a mud model, Alex," Marty said, pointing out the obvious. "It's not actually New York. I hope that was clear."

Just then, Alex had an idea. "What are we doing? Here we are, relying on the Penguins to come back for us. But you know, we've got to motivate. We should just go to Monte Carlo and get them!"

"But how do a lion, a zebra, a hippo, and a giraffe walk into a casino in Monte Carlo?" Melman asked.

"I don't know, ask the rabbi!" Marty joked.

"Hey, I'm serious," Melman shot back.

But Alex was serious, too. "Come on, we can do it," he told his friends. "We can do anything; it's us."

"We're us!" Marty agreed.

"That's right. We've gone halfway around the world," Alex reminded his friends. "Compared to that, Monte Carlo is just a hop, skip, and a swim away. To home," Alex said, raising his paw.

"To home," Marty, Melman, and Gloria agreed, raising their hooves.

"Cheeseburger!" Julien put in as he and Maurice joined their paws to the cheer.

The Zoosters said good-bye to all their friends and family in Africa. Although they were excited about the journey that lay ahead, they would miss everybody.

"I bet the Penguins will be glad to see us," Alex said.

"Yeah. They're probably bored out of their minds," Marty added.

Bored in Monte Carlo? Clearly, Alex and Marty had never been to the city. When they got there, they would find out what a wild place Monte Carlo really was.

Monte Carlo was wild, indeed. And the Penguins were having a blast! They were living in a luxury suite at a famous hotel with the Chimps, Phil and Mason. Actually, the suite didn't look so luxurious now. Piles of money and casino chips were everywhere. So were room service carts, banana peels, coffee cups, half-eaten tins of sardines and tuna, melted ice cream, and old newspapers. Disgusting!

Phil sat in front of a vanity mirror, admiring his white makeup and wig. Sticking a humanlike nose onto his face, he grinned at his reflection. In the mirror, he could see Mason swinging on a chandelier.

Meanwhile, the Penguins were having a pillow fight.

"Ha! You pillow-fight like a bunch of little girls," Skipper told Private and Kowalski.

Suddenly, Skipper was clobbered by a pillow, which exploded in a cloud of feathers.

"Chimichanga!" Skipper exclaimed. "These pillows are filled with baby birds!"

The Penguins and Chimps continued with their fun. They didn't know that they were about to get some visitors in Monte Carlo—visitors who had taken a year to reach them.

If one of the Penguins or Chimps had stopped his antics for a moment and looked out the window, he wouldn't have seen anything out of the ordinary— at least not yet. The sun was rising over the calm Mediterranean Sea. The water looked like glass, and several luxury yachts were moored in the distance.

Then, one by one, strange figures in snorkeling gear started to rise from the still water, barely creating a ripple. Who were those snorkelers? Why, they were Alex, Marty, Melman, and Gloria!

Like a periscope, Melman's head rose up. "There

it is," he mumbled through his snorkel. "The casino."

"What?" Alex mumbled, not able to make out Melman's words.

Melman took off his snorkel and repeated, "There it is. The casino!"

"Mpw the pgs," Marty heard Alex mumble through his snorkel.

"What?" Marty asked.

Alex took off his snorkel. "I said, perfect. That's where we'll find the Penguins."

"Mumble, mumble, mumble," Marty mumbled.

"What?" Gloria asked.

Marty took off his snorkel and said with a grin, "Mumble, mumble, mumble."

Gloria smacked him. This was no time to joke!

"Shhh!" Alex cautioned. "Come on, guys. Operation Penguin Extraction does not include levity. We can't draw attention to ourselves. We're invisible. I'm talking clandestine."

And with that, they submerged under the still waters of the Mediterranean Sea.

As soon as the snorkelers were gone, a swan-shaped paddleboat moved across the water. And who should be lounging on the boat but Maurice and Julien!

"Everybody, dance now!" Julien sang, swinging from the neck of the swan.

While Maurice and Julien were busy relaxing, poor little Mort was on the floor of the boat, cranking the foot pedals.

Maurice turned on music and then used a sparkler to light a bunch of fireworks.

# CHAPTER 3

It was now late in the afternoon. The group had made it to the casino and had put their plan into action.

"Okay, Phase One: We break into the casino, grab the Penguins, and get them to take us back to New York in the monkey-powered Super-Plane," Alex explained as they walked over the roof of the casino.

"Check!" Marty reported back.

"Phase Two: We berate the Penguins for abandoning us in Africa," Alex continued.

"Check!" Melman agreed.

Alex continued reciting their plan. "Phase Three: We apologize to the Penguins for the overly harsh berating, but we've gotten our point across."

"Roger that!" Gloria said.

Then Alex concluded, "Phase Four: Back to New York City."

The rest of the Zoosters excitedly agreed with that!

"All right, we take these ventilation ducts to the crawl space above the casino where we'll find the Penguins," Alex instructed, getting back to the plan. "I just need to figure out which duct each of us should take."

Actually, it was simple to figure out. One duct was long and narrow, one was wide and squat, one was striped, and one was orange—each tailor-made for a giraffe, a hippo, a zebra, and a lion!

The Zoosters traveled through their ducts until they reached a small, dusty room.

*Whoosh!* Alex flew out of his duct and shot across the room.

Then, *bang!* Marty flew out of his pipe and landed right on top of Alex!

Melman's exit was another story. He struggled to squeeze himself out from the small opening. Suddenly the wall that held the duct collapsed, and Melman shot across the room, colliding with Alex and Marty.

The three didn't have much time to think about what was happening, because at that very moment, they heard a loud rumbling noise coming from Gloria's duct.

"Uh-oh . . . ," Alex began as the rumbling got louder and louder.

Unable to move out of the way, the Zoosters did the only thing they could do—scream!

"Take cover!" Melman managed to yell as Gloria rumbled out of her duct face-first.

Then everything stopped.

Gloria was stuck!

"Hi, honey," Melman said with a sigh of relief. He untangled himself and tried to pull her out of the tube.

"Melman!" Gloria said, giggling and snorting at the same time.

"Okay," Melman said with a giggle. "Stop laughing."

As Melman tried to free Gloria from the duct, Alex and Marty worked on the plan to get into the casino, turning their attention to a piece of stained glass that was embedded into the floor in the middle of the room. Below that glass was the heart of the casino. Alex extended a claw as Marty licked his hooves and placed them on the glass. As Alex cut a circle in the glass, Marty used his hooves as suction cups to lift out the cut glass.

"Now they're not going to let animals onto the casino floor," Alex said as they peered through the glass looking for the Penguins and Chimps. "So expect some kind of disguise."

The Zoosters scanned the crowd of well-dressed, high-class gamblers below.

"Ooh, look at that!" Marty said, pointing with a hoof. "That is one ugly-magugly lady. That is roach-killing ugly!"

"That's not a lady," Alex told him. "That's the King of Versailles." He looked more closely at the person below with the white face and ugly wig and added, "And that's not the King of Versailles, that's the Chimps! And the Chimps are like smoke, and where there is smoke there is fire, and by *fire* I mean the Penguins!"

Alex was right. At the roulette table, standing in front of a big pile of chips, was the King of Versailles, who was made up of a pile of Chimps and Penguins. Phil was the face of the King, and underneath his costume were Mason, Skipper, and Kowalski. Skipper had put together a periscope so he could see what was happening at the roulette table.

"I say we let it ride," Skipper said, giving gambling instructions. "Then we'll pick up the hippies and fly back to New York in style," he continued, imagining all the money they could win.

"Can we buy an Airbus A380?" Kowalski asked.

"Solid gold, baby," Skipper told him.

Always the practical Penguin, Kowalski said, "Sir, a solid gold plane wouldn't be able to fly."

"Kowalski, we'll be rich! The rules of physics don't apply to us." Then, turning to Phil, he said, "Let it ride!"

As the Chimps and Penguins were making their bets on the casino floor, Melman had managed to pull Gloria from her duct in the ceiling.

"Okay, in exactly two minutes and seventeen

seconds, the Lemurs will cut the power," Alex instructed as he pulled out a fishing pole, a life vest, and a speargun from his duffel. "Then I drop down and grab the Penguins," he continued, attaching himself to the fishing pole. "You crank me up and we are outta here."

"Ooh! Let me drop down," Marty begged. "I'll grab the Penguins."

"You don't have fingers, Marty!" Alex told him.

Meanwhile, the Lemurs were in the control room, waiting for the exact time to pull the power switch.

"Now?" Julien asked, reaching hopefully for the switch.

"No," Maurice said, looking at his watch.

Julien stepped back, but was so anxious that he reached for the switch again. "Now?" he asked.

"No!" Maurice shouted.

"Do it?" Julien asked, not giving up.

"No," Maurice repeated.

The Lemurs weren't the only ones arguing. Up in the ceiling, Alex and Marty were yelling at each other.

"Why should you be the leader?" Marty asked Alex. "Why not me?"

"Because I'm the phase tracker!" Alex told him.

"How did I get phased out?" Marty asked.

"You're part of a phase," Alex explained. "A phase isn't something you own. It's something you're in."

"Who voted you Grand Phase Master, anyway?" Marty asked, becoming angry.

"Phase tracker!" Alex yelled, becoming exacerbated.

As the argument in the ceiling heated up, so did the action down on the casino floor.

The croupier spun the roulette wheel, and when it stopped, he was stunned.

"The King of Versailles wins it all!" the croupier shouted.

The crowd that had gathered around the table cheered as Phil grimaced a chimplike grin.

Everyone on the casino floor was happy, but the same could not be said for the group in the ceiling.

"Maybe I should be in charge," Melman said to the still arguing Marty and Alex.

"Melman!" an irritated Gloria said.

But Melman clearly thought he was right. "I am a doctor," he told them.

"Why can't we all be leaders?" Marty asked.

"Enough!" Gloria shouted. "I'm gonna lead!"

Everyone should know that you don't want to get a hippo angry. But if you do—watch out!

Gloria stomped on the glass, and—*crash!*—they all fell! Alex, who was still attached to his fishing pole pulley, hung in front of the eyes of the stunned gamblers. Below him, Gloria, Melman, and Marty lay in a pile on the smashed roulette table.

Alex spun slowly and faced a woman at the table. Nervous, Alex let out a laugh. Seeing a laughing lion staring her in the face, the woman screamed, and the panicked crowd took off!

Then, seeing Phil, Alex opened up Phil's jacket to reveal the Penguins and Mason underneath.

"What's new, pussycat?" Mason joked.

But Skipper wasn't in a joking mood; Alex had just blown their cover!

"Marty, what phase are we at?" Alex asked.

Marty hesitated for a moment, and then answered, "Phase Three."

"Phase Three," Alex repeated. Then to Skipper he said, "Hey, we are supersorry, man."

"Apology accepted," Skipper said. "Let's roll."

And with that, the Penguins took off.

"Marty! We skipped Phase Two!" Alex realized. "We didn't berate them!"

"Don't look at me," Marty told him. "You're the leader."

Back in the control room, an alarm clock sounded— an alarm clock that was taped to Mort's head.

"Yesssss!" Mort shouted as he bounced around the room.

"Now!" Maurice shouted at Julien.

"Can't you see I'm busy right now?" Julien told him.

"Just pull the switch!" Maurice shouted.

As the lights started to flicker on and off, the animals tried to make their way through the crowd. They leapfrogged, had wheelbarrow races, and carried one another, all in an attempt to escape. All through this, the lights flickered on and off.

Gloria and Melman had had enough of the flickering lights, so they went to the control room to see what was going on. There was Mort, laughing like crazy as he turned the main electrical breaker on and off. In the waves of the flashing lights, Maurice and Julien danced.

"What are you doing?" Gloria shouted.

Mort, Maurice, and Julien froze.

"Come on!" Gloria shouted at the Lemurs. Obediently, they followed her and Melman out the door.

CHAPTER 4

The Monte Carlo Casino was in a state of chaos. The guests were running and screaming for someone to save them. And who could blame them for this state of panic? After all, they were being chased by a pack of wild animals. (Or so they thought.)

"Initiate lockdown!" a security guard shouted from his hiding spot in a palm tree. "And get me Captain Dubois from Animal Control!"

Immediately, the phone in Captain Chantel Dubois's office rang.

With little sense of urgency, she reached out a gloved hand and picked up the receiver. "Speak," she said in a bored tone.

An agitated voice on the other end began to speak, slowly piquing her curiosity.

"A zebra?" she asked, more interested.

"A hippo?" she queried, even more interested now.

"A giraffe?" she said, clearly excited.

"A lion!" she exclaimed.

Hanging up the phone, Captain Dubois looked around her office—an office that was filled with stuffed and mounted heads of all sorts of animals—and spoke.

"When I was seven, I strangled my first parrot. Flushed my first goldfish. Punched my first snake." She stroked the head of a stuffed snake that was on her desk and smiled. "Now I have finally reached the moment I have been preparing for my entire life," she said as she opened up a cabinet full of weapons and traps. "The pinnacle of my career. To be tested by the king of beasts."

She pulled out a dart gun from the cabinet that was full of weapons. Then she loaded it, aimed, and shot. The dart pierced a stuffed squirrel. Then, ordering her men outside, she cocked her gun and slammed it into her holster. With a snap, she pulled on her other glove, picked up her animal catcher pole, applied her lipstick, and kick-started her moped. Captain Dubois and her Animal Control Officers were off in pursuit of the biggest catch of her life!

Back inside the casino, the animals were still trying to escape. Suddenly Alex spotted an exit—the front doors of the casino. But just as suddenly as he spotted it, thick steel shutters began to close over the doors.

"Oh no!" Alex cried in despair.

Skipper knew what was happening. "Lockdown, eh?" he stated.

"What do we do?" Melman asked worriedly.

Gloria took charge. "All right, everybody. Stand back! I've got this one."

And with that, she charged the door.

*Wham!* Gloria hit the metal door, leaving a big hippo-shaped dent.

Dazed, Gloria staggered back to join the others. "Never mind," she said.

"Well, you only get one chance at a first impression,"

Skipper joked. Then he let out a shrill whistle.

Suddenly, a sleek-looking, black armored truck plowed through the steel doors and stopped right in front of the animals. Spinning around, the back doors of the truck opened, and the animals were forced inside.

"What just happened?" Alex asked as Skipper strapped himself into a telescoping child seat command center, complete with a plastic steering wheel.

"Where are we? What is this?" Gloria wanted to know.

"We call it the Luxury Assault Recreational Vehicle, or LARV," Skipper told them as he engaged the toy plastic shift lever.

"Have a nice flight," the toy steering wheel said.

"Step on it, boys," Skipper instructed the Penguins.

Alex and Gloria turned around and saw Rico at the wheel and Private on the gas. The vehicle did a complete spin, smashed into some pillars, and then sped out the front doors of the casino.

Rico steered the vehicle right over a red Ferrari.

The luxury car exploded, and the animals' vehicle disappeared onto the streets of Monte Carlo.

Back in front of the casino, Captain Dubois led her men through the smoke and destruction. A panicked casino security officer ran up to her and said, "Captain Dubois! I am so happy to see you. You will not believe—"

Dubois grabbed him by the collar and slapped him several times.

"Get back, you fool!" she said between slaps. "Your cheap cologne is obscuring the animal musk."

"Ow, my face!" the officer moaned, rubbing the spot where Dubois hit him.

Unapologetic about her behavior, Dubois just tossed the man aside, dropped to the pavement, and started sniffing like a dog.

As she crawled across the road, she picked up the scent. One of her men leaned in to look, but another Animal Control Officer slapped him. After all, that man should have known to leave the captain alone while she was working!

"Poor, poor animals," Capitain Dubois said with a crazed look on her face. "You should have never left the forest. Now you deal with me!"

As Captain Dubois was trying to pick up their scent, the Zoosters were speeding down the streets of Monte Carlo in the LARV.

"Kowalski, signal the Chimps to meet us at the rendezvous point with the Super-Plane," Skipper ordered.

Obediently, Kowalski pushed a button next to the radar display.

Skipper continued with his orders. "Hotel Ambassador. Let's move it!"

"Woo-hoo! Yeah!" Melman shouted, his long neck and head sticking out of the vehicle's window. He was clearly enjoying the ride until—*bang!*—he hit a street sign. Ouch!

Suddenly, Melman picked up the sound of a siren. "Guys, we've got a tail!" he said, catching sight of the Animal Control scooters.

"Paparazzi!" Julien cried.

"Pedal to the metal, Private," Skipper ordered.

Immediately, Private threw his body on the gas pedal, and Rico steered wildly, trying to avoid the oncoming traffic.

Julien, who thought photographers were pursuing them, opened up the back door and struck a pose.

"Don't take any photos," Julien said. "Please, here I am."

Seeing Julien hanging out the back door was just too good to be true for Captain Dubois. She raised her gun and fired a tranquilizer dart.

The dart hit Julien right in the butt! "Don't take any photos . . . ," he began, feeling drowsy from the tranquilizer.

Then he collapsed!

"Medic!" Skipper called out as more darts flew through the air.

"No more pictures," Mort said as he and Maurice shut the rear doors.

Skipper pulled out the dart from Julien's behind and inspected it. Then, getting back to business, he said, "ETA to the rendezvous point?"

"Two minutes, thirty-seven seconds, sir!" Kowalski reported, checking the display.

Skipper rang a little bell on the steering wheel. "Man your battle stations," he ordered the Penguins.

Private and Rico left their driving posts and manned their battle stations.

"Hey, wait! Nobody's at the wheel!" Alex said, panicked. "Get back there!"

But no one listened to him as the vehicle veered to the side of the road and sideswiped the parked cars.

Now Marty, Melman, and Gloria were panicking, too. Without a driver, they were sure to crash!

Skipper turned to Alex and said, "Don't just sit there, fancy-pants! Grab the wheel!"

"Are you kidding?" Alex told him. "I don't drive. I'm a New Yorker."

"Move over, Miss Daisy," Marty said, pushing his way to the front. He hopped into the driver's seat and hit the gas.

"What are you doing?" Alex cried. "Zebras can't drive. Only Penguins and people can drive!"

But Marty wasn't listening. "What do all these buttons do?" he asked excitedly. Recklessly, he started pushing the buttons in front of him.

Marty was having fun being in control of the wheel. He swerved to avoid some traffic, drove up the back of a hatchback, and did a 360-barrel roll that landed them back in the middle of the street.

"Nice one, stripes," Skipper complimented him.

But Skipper was the only one who liked Marty's driving. Everyone else—inside and outside the vehicle—was scared for his or her lives.

"Crazy woman gaining!" Maurice shouted as he watched Captain Dubois riding furiously toward them.

"Our Omega-3 slick will take them down!" Skipper said, thinking of a way to stop Dubois and her men. "Private, activate!"

Immediately, Private pulled a lever and a pile of slippery mackerel dumped out onto the road.

Seeing the fish, Dubois and her men leaped off their scooters and lifted them over their heads. Then they slid their way through the oily mackerel.

Suddenly, a car pulled out from a side street. Without missing a beat, Dubois flipped over the hood of the car, landing on the other side and right back on her scooter!

"She's good," Skipper remarked, impressed with the captain's moves.

The chase was back on, and the LARV squealed around a corner, racing along the waterfront. Just then, two of Dubois's officers swerved to avoid an oncoming car and—*splash!*—landed in the water. Unfazed, the captain continued her pursuit.

Marty was having a blast at the wheel. He steered the vehicle into a tunnel, then down a one-way street. (Down the *wrong* way, that is!)

"You're going the wrong way, Marty!" Alex shouted.

"Just call me Marty-O Andretti!" Marty yelled.

"No, you're Sucky-o Andretti!" Alex corrected.

"Stop backseat driving," Marty told Alex.

"I'm passenger-seat driving," Alex said, "and I want the wheel. Give me the wheel!"

"It's not a wheel," Marty said. "It's my baby."

"Your hooves aren't meant to be on a wheel," Alex told him.

"Hey, too late for you to drive," Marty said.

"Don't look at me when we argue, look at the road," Alex shot back.

Marty and Alex were so busy arguing that they didn't notice that Dubois had pulled right up to their window. Finally, out of the corner of his eye, Marty noticed the captain.

"Be cool, be cool," he told himself. "Hi, Officer, is there a problem?" he asked.

"Hi," Alex echoed nervously.

Dubois answered them with a scowl and a raised dart gun.

"She's got a gun, she's got a gun, she's got a gun!" Gloria shouted, noticing the armed captain.

"Watch out!" Melman cried.

Just then, a car zoomed toward Dubois, momentarily distracting her. Dubois flew over the top of the oncoming car and landed on the bumper of the animals' vehicle. With incredible strength, Dubois climbed to the top of the vehicle and tried to force her way inside.

"We need more power!" Skipper ordered. "Time to fire up Kowalski's nucular reactor." He pushed a button, and floor panels slid away revealing an ominous-looking device.

"That's a nuclear reactor?" Gloria asked incredulously.

"Nucular," Skipper repeated.

Melman tried to warn them that Dubois was on the roof, but no one listened.

Kowalski looked at the device. "But, sir, it's not ready," he warned. "The control rods will have to be calibrated. And don't even ask me about the Uranium-238 blanket."

Skipper listened to Kowalski complain, but he

was also watching Dubois, and she was about to rip off the roof!

"Okay," Skipper said to Kowalski, just to placate him. But as he spoke, he switched on the reactor.

An eerie glow emanated from the device.

Then they heard the whine of an engine and—*whoosh!*—the LARV jetted away. And with that, Dubois fell off the roof and was left behind.

## CHAPTER 6

With Dubois off their tails, the Zoosters
continued their escape.

"Okay, Marty," Alex said. "We lost her, maybe you
can slow down."

Marty shook his head. "I can't. There's no brakes!"

"No brakes?" Skipper asked Kowalski.

Kowalski shrugged.

"Well, way to commit, soldier," Skipper said,
beaming with pride.

Marty continued to steer the vehicle. Suddenly
they saw a wall of road barriers in front of them. They
were barreling toward a construction site and had no
way to stop! The workmen at the site dived out of the

way, and the animals inside the LARV screamed at the top of their lungs. This was it, they all thought; for at the end of the construction site there was a railing and then nothing—nothing except a long, long drop!

The LARV reached the end of the railing and launched into the air.

"Aaaagh!" the animals screamed.

Then, with a bump, the LARV landed on top of the roof of the Hotel Ambassador. The animals froze in terror as they stared out the window at the ten-story drop.

"Let's get outta here!" Alex cried as their vehicle teetered on the roof.

The animals scrambled out the back of the LARV. They were all safe—all except Julien, who was lounging against the reactor.

"Hey, where is everybody going?" he asked.

But as soon as the words were out of his mouth, the LARV fell over the edge, taking Julien with it!

The animals were horrified. Julien was gone! Mort started to cry. (But Maurice tried to hide his smile.)

Suddenly they heard a rumbling noise. Cautiously, the group looked over the edge and saw the LARV magically rising up!

"I'm flying, I'm flying!" Julien shouted with glee. "I'm the first flying monkey!"

Sure enough, Julien *was* flying. He was resting on the tail of a monkey-powered Super-Plane!

Seeing Julien, the Zoosters cheered. (Except for Maurice, that is!)

The plane hovered above them, and a chain of Chimps dropped down.

"That's our ticket outta here!" Marty said excitedly.

"Yeah, baby!" Melman cheered. He and the other animals were thrilled—this *was* their way back home to New York City!

They heard the buzz of another engine. Turning around, they saw Dubois on her scooter, exploding out of a door on the neighboring rooftop! With a determined look in her eyes, she launched her scooter into the air. But the gap between the two buildings was wide—too wide for her to make it across, right?

As Captain Dubois flew, she tried to remain calm. Up, up, and then over, over, down . . . at the last second, Dubois abandoned her scooter and launched her body toward the rooftop.

Seeing that Dubois was nearing, Alex cried, "Everybody, on the monkey chain!"

The Zoosters scrambled toward the Chimps as Dubois landed on the rooftop. Ready for battle, she pulled out a telescoping snare.

"Deploy banana gun!" Skipper shouted up to the plane.

As soon as the order was shouted, a chimp-manned banana gun dropped out of the plane and opened fire on Dubois. As she dodged the bananas, the Zoosters raced to grab onto the chain. They hoped the bananas would buy them time to board the plane.

"Grab the little guys!" Alex cried, motioning to the smaller animals. "Toss 'em up! Let's go! Go, go, go!"

Alex and Gloria grabbed the smaller animals and tossed them up on the chain, and then everyone grabbed on.

"C'mon, Melman!" Alex shouted as he helped Melman to the bottom of the chain.

"Woo! Yeah!" Melman shouted as he hung on.

Just then, Dubois swung her snare, and it landed around Melman's neck—just like a rope noose!

"Aaaack!" Melman cried as he was pulled off the chain.

"Melman!" Gloria shouted in distress.

Quickly, Alex grabbed Melman's hoof, but then *he* got pulled off the chain. The last Chimp on the chain reached out to Alex.

As Alex yanked on Melman's hoof, Dubois pulled on the noose.

"My neck!" Melman cried out, trying to free himself from Dubois's trap.

Meanwhile, Skipper and the other smaller animals managed to make their way safely to the plane. Skipper looked down and saw Alex and Melman struggling. "Put your backs into it!" he ordered the Chimps. "Double banana overtime!"

And with that, the Chimp pilot pulled a lever and

a ton of bananas flew out and pelted Dubois.

Suddenly the concrete beneath Dubois's feet crumbled, and she was pulled off the building. Still ever determined, she held on tightly to her end of the rope. Now Melman was carrying the weight of Dubois around his neck!

"Serpentine! Serpentine!" Skipper ordered.

The Chimps cranked wildly on the plane's steering wheel. The plane banked left and right, yet Dubois hung on. Then *crash!* Capitain Dubois smacked into an office building and lost her grip on the snare.

But Dubois wasn't finished. She scrambled to her feet and dashed inside the building. She sprinted through the offices, leaped over desks, slid across conference tables, all the while keeping pace with the plane that was flying outside the office window. Finally, she burst out the opposite side of the building and grabbed the end of the noose that was still dangling from Melman's neck!

"Hey, this lady's really starting to freak me out," Julien said as he watched Dubois start to climb up the rope. "Fix it, Mort," he commanded. And with that, he kicked poor little Mort out the plane's door!

Mort landed smack on Dubois's face and quickly dived into her shirt.

"Ack!" Dubois cried as Mort tickled her.

Alex knew it was time for him to take charge. "Hold this," he said, handing a Chimp Melman's hoof. Then he climbed down Melman's neck toward his head.

"Alex, be careful!" Marty cried. "She's crazy!"

"You think, Marty?" Alex said.

Dubois was ready for a fight. She held on tightly to the rope and climbed up toward Melman's head. But just as she was about to reach Melman, Mort jumped out of her shirt and onto her hat, and then scrambled up the chain. Seeing that Dubois was momentarily distracted, Alex reached out and sliced Dubois's noose with his claw.

Dubois fell and splashed into a rooftop pool below.

"I can breathe! I can breathe!" Melman shouted, holding his hooves to his neck.

"Bye," Mort called down to Dubois.

"That's right. Home free, baby!" Alex shouted, knowing that they could now head to New York.

Down below, a soaking wet Dubois emerged from the pool. Looking at the plane overhead, she said, "Well played, lion. Game on."

Clearly the chase was not over.

CHAPTER 7

The Super-Plane flapped its wings and flew smoothly across the sky. Inside the plane, the animals were celebrating their escape. Alex, Melman, Marty, and Gloria were singing a corny song that was clearly driving Skipper crazy.

"Kowalski, status report," Skipper said, rolling his eyes at the Zoosters.

"The good news is, this song is almost over," Kowalski reported.

"Well, that's music to my ears," Skipper responded. "And the bad news?"

"The gear assembly is badly damaged," Kowalski told him.

As soon as Kowalski said that, the cotter pin, which is used to keep parts safely in place, fell out of the plane's main axle. And if that wasn't bad enough, the gear fell out and bounced around the fuselage. It bounced and bounced and bounced until *boom!* It hit Alex on his head and knocked him out cold!

"It's only a matter of time before—"

But before Kowalski could finish his sentence, the plane spiraled down out of control!

Down, down, down, the Super-Plane plummeted and crash-landed in the middle of a train yard somewhere in the south of France.

"Why can't we ever just make a normal landing?" Melman asked, hanging upside down from the tail section of the plane.

"Oh, man," Alex said, opening his eyes and surveying the mess of twisted metal that surrounded them. He sat up, turned around, and saw Gloria getting to her feet. Underneath her were a couple of crushed (but don't worry, uninjured) Chimps.

"Hold on, Melman! I'll get you down, sweetie,"

Gloria said. She lumbered over and helped Melman down from the wreckage.

"Where is he?" Mort cried, staggering around, his arms and body stuck inside a pipe. "Must find King Julien!"

Just then, he spotted Julien, who was stumbling away from the wreckage and singing a very silly song.

Desperately, Alex turned to Skipper. "Skipper, what about the plane?" he asked.

Skipper hopped down parts of the broken aircraft and slid down a pipe. "Well, the Chimps will work through the night," he reported. "No breaks. No safety restrictions."

But the Chimps weren't listening to what Skipper was saying—they were leaving!

"Hey, where're ya going?" Skipper called after them.

One of the Chimps stopped and thumbed his nose at Skipper in reply.

"Get back here!" Skipper shouted. "We have a contract!"

"Yes, well, I'm afraid labor laws are slightly more

lenient in France," Mason told him. "You see, they only have to work two weeks a year."

"Well, someone else has the Canadian work ethic," Skipper told him.

Melman was starting to panic. (Well, he was panicking before, but he was panicking even more now!) "But you Penguins, you can still fix it, right?" he asked Skipper.

"Yeah, yeah! You're a little cracker-jack can-do team!" Alex put in.

Skipper looked at them. "You want me to give it to you straight?" he asked.

"Yes, yes . . . no. Bend it a little," Alex said nervously.

"Well, the plane's totaled," Skipper said, giving them the entire truth. "Blammo. Busted. Never to fly again," he added, rubbing it in.

"So what, that's it?" a defeated Gloria asked. "That's it then," she said, answering her own question.

But Alex wasn't about to give up. "No, we gotta get home. We can fix it! We'll fix it! Yeah, guys, c'mon, we'll fix it!"

Alex started to pick up random pieces of the broken plane and tried to jam them together.

"You just start from the outside pieces and you work your way in," Alex rambled. "And yeah . . . perfect. Come on, don't just stand there, guys! Marty! Drag that thingy over here, and we'll just attach it to this little dealy-bop over here, and—"

"Alex," Marty said, trying to stop his friend.

Just then, the pieces that Alex were jamming together crashed down. Alex was finally defeated. "We're not going home. We're never going home," he stated.

Gloria reached out and touched Alex's shoulder, trying to comfort him.

But there was no time to cry, for just at that moment, police sirens blared.

"It's the fuzz!" Marty shouted.

Desperately, the animals dashed through the train yard.

"What are we gonna do?" Marty asked. "We can't hide forever!"

"And we can't just blend. You know this isn't Africa," Gloria added.

Suddenly, Melman stopped running. "What's the point?" he asked.

The animals turned back to Melman. What was he doing? This was the *wrong* time to complain!

"Tell me one conceivable way that extra-large animals like us are going to be able to move through Europe without attracting unwanted attention?"

But no one answered him, because they were all too busy staring at a train car with a big circus logo. They leaned in for a closer look.

Suddenly, the boxcar swung open, revealing a *huge* tiger!

"Aaagh!" they all screamed.

"Where are you coming from?" the tiger asked them, anger in his voice.

"Please. You gotta hide us," Alex bravely requested. "Just until the heat dies down."

"Absolut no outsiders. So wipe that Smirnoff your face and Popov!" the tiger replied.

"Oh, c'mon, man. You got to do one cat a solid. Cat to cat," Alex said. "Do us a solid here, buddy. C'mon. Till the heat dies down . . ."

"Nyet!" the tiger answered. "This train is for circus animals only." And with that, he slammed the door shut.

The Zoosters stood outside the circus car, stunned. What were they going to do? If the circus animals didn't take them in, the police would capture them. Then what? The animals shuddered at the thought.

"They sound like they're in trouble," the Zoosters heard a voice say from inside the train car.

"Stefano, we do not invite trouble into our circus," the tiger said. "I don't trust lion, hair too big and glossy."

"Come on, Vitaly, you're being mean," Stefano said.

"He not lion, he lioness with a beehive!" Vitaly responded.

"I'm just saying that if they are in trouble, we do not leave them out there," Stefano told the tiger.

"This is awkward," Alex told the Zoosters. "We can hear everything they're saying."

"It is not our problem," Vitaly declared.

"But, Vitaly . . . ," Stefano tried to reason.

"Nyet, nyet!" Vitaly said.

Suddenly the train lurched forward. It was leaving!

"No, no, no. Wait, wait, wait!" Alex called out after the train.

Just then, the train door opened, and the head of a big sea lion popped out. It was Stefano. "Eh, give us a minute," Stefano told the Zoosters. "He's on the phone. I can't get him off." And with that, he pulled his head back into the train car and shut the door.

The Zoosters heard Stefano and Vitaly arguing.

"We cannot leave them there!" Stefano implored.

"Only circus animals on this train," Vitaly told him.

Alex banged on the door. "Wait! Listen. We *are* circus animals! You gotta let us in!"

The train door slid open again. "You are really circus?" a beautiful jaguar asked.

"Yes! Full circus," Alex told her. "Totally circus."

Melman, Marty, and Gloria agreed. "Absolutely. To the core. My momma was circus. My daddy was circus."

The animals pleaded their case as they ran alongside the moving train. At the same time, the police were getting closer. Radios squawked and flashlight beams raked over and under the trains. If the circus animals didn't let them on in the next minute, they'd be found!

"Gia, close the door," Vitaly ordered the jaguar.

"Please," Gloria whispered, hoping that Vitaly would finally give in and save them.

"They are circus," Gia begged Vitaly. "Circus sticks together."

Vitaly sighed. Gia was right. If those animals outside were circus, it was his duty to help them. He nodded to Gia, and she held out her hand.

The Zoosters were saved! Quickly, they all scrambled onto the moving train. The doors shut just as the police leveled their flashlight beams on the train. The Circus Train chugged out of the yard as the police continued their search. The Zoosters were safe.

Safe for now, that is.

# CHAPTER 8

The inside of the train car was dark. Stefano lit a lantern. Gia and Vitaly were on one side of the car, and the Zoosters were huddled together on the opposite side. Everyone sat in silence.

"Wow! Circus Americano!" Stefano said, breaking the ice. "You must all be very famous!"

The Zoosters did not know what to say. Marty and Alex stuttered a response, and Gloria confidently added, "Absolutely!"

"We're relatively well-known in all the—" Alex started.

"But Alex is really the star," Marty put in.

"Yeah. Well, I wouldn't say star," Alex said

modestly. "More like . . ." He thought a moment, then conceded. "The star."

Vitaly, who was twirling a knife in his paws, stopped to listen.

"What is your act, Alice?" Stefano asked Alex.

Alex tried to think fast. "Well, I basically . . . I jump up on my rock . . ."

"Rock?" Gia interrupted.

"It's a very high rock," Alex told her.

"And then?" Stefano wanted to know.

"And then . . . I . . . well, I roar, like a serious *RAWR!*" Alex said.

"And then?" Stefano wanted more.

Alex was confused. What more could there be? A roar was a roar! That was his whole show!

Alex had to think of something to say. "And then I jump off the rock," he added.

"And then?" Stefano asked, still wanting more.

*And then. And then what?* Alex wondered. What exactly did these circus animals want to hear?

"Into a pool!" Gloria added.

"Full of acid!" Marty put in.

"Full of cobras!" Melman said to add more danger.

"Actually, it appears like I'm jumping into a pool full of acid," Alex said.

"And cobras," Melman said, not wanting his idea to be forgotten.

"Aquatic cobras . . . for effect," Alex told them. "But I actually pull up at the last second."

The circus animals did not know what he meant by *pull up*. "How do you do that?" Stefano wanted to know.

The Zoosters were stumped. How *would* Alex get out of that one? They each had different ideas—a parachute, a wire harness, a balloon, a jet pack.

"Well, wire harness suspended from a jet pack while I toss balloons to the children of the world," Alex said, putting all the ideas together. Then he added, "Kids love it. Kids always love that."

"Hmph!" a disbelieving Vitaly said.

But Stefano was confused. He did not understand what Alex had described, since he had never seen anything like that before. "Is this like the trapeze?" he asked.

58

"Yes! Trapeze! Exactly!" Alex shouted.

Stefano was impressed. "Wow! Trapeze Americano! Hey! I have a great idea! Maybe you can come with us to Roma?"

But before Alex could answer—*thunk!* A dagger landed in the wall an inch from Stefano's face.

"Vitaly is just playing around," Stefano said, hanging his lantern on the dagger handle.

"Yeah, thanks. Thanks," Alex told Stefano. "But we'll get off at the next stop so we can get back to America. You know. Without multiple stab wounds," he said, referring to Vitaly's antics.

"That is such a coincidence!" Stefano exclaimed. "Because we're going to—"

*Thunk!* Another dagger flew into the wall, missing Stefano's face by inches again.

Clearly, Stefano did not understand that Vitaly was trying to get him to keep quiet. It was enough that they were giving the Zoosters a ride, but take them to Rome or to America? Not if Vitaly could help it.

But Stefano kept divulging their travel plans. Each

time he did, Vitaly flung another knife in his direction.

"You're going to America?" Gloria asked as Melman, Alex, and Marty grew more and more excited.

Vitaly's eyes darted around the room. He was becoming really angry now.

"*Sì!*" Stefano answered. "After Roma, we go to London. And big-time promoter will see us and then send us to New York."

"Guys! They're going to New York!" Alex exclaimed.

"Well, only if he likes what he sees," Gia put in.

The Zoosters were seriously excited now. New York was their home, and that was where the circus animals were heading!

"Could we go with you?" Marty asked.

"Sure! You can bunk with Vitaly!" Stefano answered.

*Thunk!* A battle-ax hit the wall next to Stefano. *Whack!* A dagger hit the wall next to Gia's head. *Thwap!* A sword swung above Gloria's head. *Sprong!* A double-bladed knife pinned Melman's neck. *Thap! Thap!* Two axes pinned Marty's head. Then *thuka!* A spear flew between Alex's legs.

"Whoa," Alex said, looking at all the deadly weapons.

"Or not," Stefano finally conceded.

Quietly, Vitaly stepped into the light. *"Nyet"* was all he said as he strode past Stefano toward the Zoosters' end of the boxcar.

"Oh no," Stefano said. "I don't think Vitaly likes that idea! What's he gonna do?"

"Which one of you is leader?" Vitaly asked the Zoosters.

Marty smiled and gestured to Alex.

"Tell your comrades, there is one rule we do not break," Vitaly addressed Alex.

"Thou shall say it and not spray it?" Alex joked.

*"Nyet!"* Vitaly shouted. "Circus owner no allow stowaways."

Just then, a chain saw blade dropped down from above. The blade stopped inches from Vitaly's face and circled him. And then the Penguins fell to the floor on a chunk of ceiling.

"I hear you, Russki!" Skipper said, addressing Vitaly. "Although the circus owner may allow

61

stowaways if the stowaways just happen to be the owner. Riddle me that."

"What is sharply dressed little birdie talking about?" Vitaly asked, gesturing toward Skipper.

"Show 'em, boys," Skipper said.

Up on the roof of the train, the Chimps were putting their plan into action. Phil (dressed as the King of Versailles) picked up an elegant-looking purse and shook it. Jewels and gold rattled inside.

Moments later, the Chimps were off the train, and Phil dumped the diamonds and gold onto a circus crate. On the other side of the crate was the Circus Master; his eyes grew wide at the sight of the fortune before him. Behind him, a circus clown snickered.

"You have a deal, *mi amigo*," the Circus Master said as he placed the deed to the circus on the crate.

The deal was made. The King of Versailles had bought the circus! The Circus Master and his clowns climbed into a tiny car. They couldn't believe their luck—they had gotten rid of their lousy circus and had gotten a fortune in return! The clowns were laughing;

what a fool this king was.

"I am sure this circus will bring you great success," the Circus Master lied, trying to keep his clowns quiet.

"I guess this is good-bye," he continued, trying not to laugh. "And good luck," he said, finally breaking down.

And with that, the hysterical Circus Master and his clowns drove away.

Just then, the Zoosters opened up one of the doors to the train cars. Mason gave a thumbs-up. Seeing this, the Zoosters knew the deal had been made. Skipper's riddle had been solved—they were the owners of the circus now!

"There's nothing left for us to do but ride this Circus Train all the way to New York," Alex concluded.

And that was exactly the plan.

## CHAPTER 9

The Zoosters and the circus animals sat in the train as it chugged toward Rome. Who was driving the train? Why, the Penguins, of course! And they were having lots of fun. As the train picked up speed, they pulled whistles and opened steam valves.

Meanwhile, the Lemurs bounced along the top of the train cars. Wanting to explore, Maurice and Mort jumped down into a boxcar, and Julien quickly followed.

"Hey, this is not first class," Julien said, sniffing around.

"Definitely coach," Maurice commented, looking at a chewed up tire that hung on a rope.

As the Lemurs walked around the car, they saw

that the walls were covered in giant claw marks. Metal hooks dangled from the ceiling.

Suddenly, they stepped on something crunchy. Looking down, they saw fish bones and fish heads littering the floor. Screaming, they ran for cover. What kind of place was this?

Then they heard a low grumble and saw a pair of glowing red eyes in the far corner of the car. Shaking with fear, the Lemurs watched as a huge black bear emerged from the shadows. But this wasn't any bear— it was a circus bear riding a tricycle. Still, the bear looked scary. (And the drool dripping off her muzzle didn't help!)

Julien gazed at the massive beast. But instead of running away in fear, Julien fell in love!

"Hey, gorgeous," Julien began. "Has anyone ever told you that you look like a supermodel? Albeit a fat, hairy one who smells."

In response, the bear picked up Julien in her mouth. Then she put him on her back and started to bob for fish.

"Oooh. You have a very hairy back. I like that in a woman," Julien said, running his fingers through the bear's fur.

The bear growled happily.

As the Zoosters were making their getaway on the Circus Train, the police were investigating the scene of the Super-Plane crash. They stood behind yellow caution tape and took photographs, bagging the evidence they could reach.

"That's it. I'm going in," one of the policemen declared.

The other policemen tried to tell him it was too dangerous and warned him not to cross the yellow tape.

Not listening, the policeman went over the caution tape and stepped into the wreckage. *Whoosh!* He slipped and fell on a banana peel! Then he got up and fell again!

But there was someone who had managed to cross the yellow caution tape. Someone who was checking out every part of the wreckage. Someone who was sniffing the ground and lapping up water from a paw print. Someone who had just picked up a scent.

That someone was Captain Dubois!

"Lion, twelve hours old, two hundred and fifty kilograms, glossy mane, too much conditioner," Dubois declared.

Dubois sniffed her way over to the tracks that the Circus Train had been on. She sniffed and sniffed and sniffed. Then she saw! She saw the trail that the Zoosters left behind as they hopped aboard the Circus Train.

"Hello, kitty," Dubois said as she reapplied her bright-red lipstick. "So you have run away with the circus. What a cliché."

Suddenly, a train came barreling down the track. And it was headed straight for her! Without batting an eyelash, Dubois dropped down and lay flat between the rails. As the train plowed over her, she rolled between the train's wheels to the side of the tracks and leaped aboard. Satisfied, Captain Dubois smiled. She was headed to Rome!

Inside the ancient Colosseum in Rome, a big circus
tent was set up. Customers lined up to buy their tickets,
excited for the show. Mason, who wore clown makeup
and a fake nose, took the money and handed the people
their tickets. A few were surprised at the ticket taker's
hairy hands, but this *was* the circus after all. Mason
passed the money below the ticket booth, where the
Penguins were busy at work. Kowalski poured the money
into Rico's mouth and then he spit it out in rolled-up bills.

"What a dump," Skipper said, referring to the
Colosseum. "If they want to attract a decent sports
team, they should bulldoze this rattrap and invest in a
new arena."

68

As the Chimps and Penguins were working the sales, the larger animals strolled around backstage.

"The Colosseum, Marty!" Alex said, gesturing grandly. "The original theater in the round. You know, my ancestors used to perform here."

"No kidding?" Marty remarked.

"Every show had a captive audience. Apparently they killed," Alex told him. He was talking about the time when the gladiators fought lions—to the death.

"Sounds like a great gig," Marty said, not understanding the history of the place.

Marty and Alex opened a curtain and continued walking through the backstage area, which was bustling with activity as the animals got ready for the show. All around them, animals were stretching, putting on costumes, and warming up for their acts.

"*Tre minuti*, everybody! *Tre minuti*!" Stefano shouted as he ran through the crowd.

"This is so exciting!" Marty said, his eyes wide as he looked around.

"Remember, we just lie low," Alex warned. "Stay

out of the way. Let them do their thing." The last thing Alex wanted was to be part of the show.

Marty didn't answer Alex; he was too busy looking at a group of little terriers dressed up in top hats and chiffon dresses.

"Aw, will you look at this!" he said as he watched the innocent-looking dogs practice their dance steps. "You gotta go back inside your mama's belly, 'cause you're too cute to be out here in the real world right now," Marty continued in a baby voice.

"Naff off, you muppet!" one of the dogs barked at Marty.

Another dog pulled out a chain, another whipped out a switchblade, and another dog broke a bottle and held it out, threatening Marty.

Too cute? Think again!

"What the . . . ," Marty said as he backed into Alex.

"Marty, they're professionals, come on," Alex tried to explain.

Alex left Marty behind as he went to address the elephants.

"All right, animals. We may be your new owners, but we don't want to reinvent the circus wheel here, right?" Alex told them. "So just go out and do what you do. Just think of this as a warm-up for that promoter in London. Right, Marty?" Alex looked around for Marty, but couldn't find him. "Marty?" he called.

Then he spotted Marty.

"I want to be a circus horse," Marty said, admiring himself in a mirror.

"Not lying very low, are we, Marty?" Alex said as he approached the group.

"Okay, okay," Marty told Alex. Then, turning back to the horses, he said, "Anyway, ladies, as I was trying to say before we were so rudely interrupted—"

But Marty was interrupted again. This time by Stefano, who was running around looking for Sonya the bear.

Alex sighed and kept walking through the backstage. He passed Vitaly, who was leaning against a tent pole and eating a bowl of borscht.

"Hey, Vitaly. Got your game face on?" Alex remarked, giving him a thumbs-up.

Vitaly snarled in response.

"Great! Good game face!" Alex said, moving on. "What is that cat's problem? *I am a mean Russian cat who isn't nice to anybody*," Alex said, mimicking Vitaly.

Just then, Alex spotted Gloria and Melman. Melman was trying to juggle bowling pins and Gloria was wearing Sonya's tutu and dancing in front of a mirror.

"Hey, honey!" Melman shouted to Gloria. "Look! I'm doing it!"

Gloria turned to look at Melman. And Melman dropped the pins!

"Guys, stop fooling around," Alex told them.

"We're just having a little fun," Melman said.

"Let's let these animals do their show," Alex cautioned. The last thing he wanted was for himself and his friends to *really* join the circus.

Suddenly, Stefano ran past shouting for Sonya the bear again. Where was she?

The only one who knew where to find Sonya was Julien. That was because he was with her!

Julien and Sonya were having a blast riding around Rome. Julien stole the Pope's ring and presented it to Sonya. Then the pair rubbed their backs against some ancient columns and ran away laughing. *Crash!* The columns tumbled down behind them.

"I want to kiss every inch of your huge head," Julien said, grabbing Sonya's face, "which may take me a number of weeks."

He leaned forward to kiss her, but before he could make his move, they tumbled down a set of stairs.

"Hey, wow!" Julien cried out as he lay squashed beneath Sonya at the bottom of the stairs.

Sonya sat up, held out the broken pieces of her tricycle, and started to cry.

"That was heavy," Julien said.

Sonya looked sadly at Julien.

"Stop crying," Julien said, grabbing her face. "It makes me cry to see you cry, my darling. I will get you something even better."

Julien led her to a fancy motorcycle store. They hopped on a Ducati bike and roared out of the dealership, sending people running in fear.

"Hey, you *can* buy love!" Julien shouted. He looked back at the owner of the store, who was holding pieces of the tricycle and the gold ring.

Moments later, the police raced in and pointed their guns at the Ducati dealer. The Pope's gold ring was recovered!

As Julien and Sonya wreaked havoc through Rome, Alex continued to walk around backstage making sure all the animals were ready for the show.

"Ladies and gentlemen, presenting Gia the trapeze-flying jaguar," Alex heard someone say.

He looked around and saw the outline of a figure behind a screen. Quietly, he approached and saw that it was Gia. Alex smiled.

"And here she does the triple flip roll with a double leap," Gia said as she rolled and flipped.

Alex leaned in and watched her practice her trapeze act.

Then *riiip!* Alex tore through the screen and fell at Gia's feet!

"What are you doing?" a surprised Gia asked.

"That screen is just paper," Alex commented, gesturing to where he fell. Immediately, he hopped up and faced Gia, their faces nearly touching.

"Were you spying on me?" Gia accused.

"No, no, no!" Alex said, trying to sound confident. "I just came by to say that I don't want you to—"

*Riiip!* Alex fell through another piece of paper screen and fell to the ground—again!

Without missing a beat, he stood up. "I don't want you to think of me as some sort of authority figure."

*Crash!* Alex leaned up against a rack of hanging rings and pulled the whole thing down!

"Don't worry, I don't," Gia said as she watched Alex pick up the rings.

"You don't? Oh," Alex said, sounding a bit disappointed.

"Not at all," Gia assured him.

"Well, the other circus animals might find me a

bit intimidating," Alex explained.

"No, nobody is intimidated at all by you," Gia replied.

"Oh. Good stuff. Good, good news," Alex said.

"In fact," Gia said, narrowing her eyes, "I don't think they have given you a second thought since you showed up."

Alex's feelings were bruised, but he wasn't going to let Gia know that. Instead, he said, "That's good to hear." And he started to hang up the fallen rings.

"If anything, they are starting to feel sorry for you," Gia admitted.

"All right!" Alex said, unable to contain his emotions any longer. "I get it!" He fumbled with the rings and one fell from his paws. Alex and Gia both leaned in to pick up the ring and—*clonk!*—they banged heads.

"Is there more?" Gia asked, growing irritated.

"I just wanted to thank you for letting us get on the train back there," Alex told her. Then he continued in a Russian accent, "I know the big cat with the accent wasn't too excited by us getting on the train."

Gia threw a hoop around Alex's neck and pulled

him close. "Look, Lion Guy. This circus means everything to us. And if you do anything that threatens this circus or a single hair of any animal in it, you will have to answer to me, capiche?"

"Capiche," Alex agreed. Alex leaned against a cable wire, and the wall collapsed! As the wall fell, his leg got caught in a rope, and he swung up. But before he could fall, Gia caught him.

Just then, Marty walked in. *What are those two doing?* he wondered. *It looks like they are hugging!*

"You call this lying low?" Marty asked Alex.

And with that, Gia dropped Alex on the ground.

While the animals were frantically getting ready
for the circus, Julien and Sonya were happily riding all
over Rome. Now they were heading for a train yard.
They ramped over a parked car and onto the roof
of a truck. Finally, they landed on the ground. Still
moving, they slid under the train gate arm just as it
was coming down and rode over the tracks seconds
before a train whizzed by.

"Faster! Faster! Whoa!" Julien said as they did
tricks on their motorcycle.

They were having so much fun that they didn't
care if anyone was watching them. But they should
have been paying more attention, for standing in the

shadows was Captain Dubois!

"Where there is smoke, there is *lion*!" Dubois said as she watched the animals ride by. She put on a coat of lipstick and said, "When in Rome . . ." And she jumped on a nearby Vespa. "Vive la France!" she said, kick-starting the bike.

As she took off after Julien and Sonya, her eyes widened. Her Vespa was chained to an entire line of other Vespas!

"*Halta!*" a policeman shouted as he ran toward her. He jumped onto another chained Vespa and took off after Dubois.

Dubois rode her bike as far as the chain stretched, and then she was launched into the air. She flew over the heads of Julien and Sonya as they were drinking from a fountain and landed in the water.

"Come on, my hairy queen, we'll do doughnuts in the Pantheon," Julien said, not noticing Dubois.

Dubois raised her gun to shoot them, but just as she was about to pull the trigger, a pair of handcuffs was thrown on her wrists!

"You are in big trouble!" a policeman told her.

Dubois fired her gun at the officer and a tranquilizer dart hit him. *Splash!* He fell into the fountain.

A second policeman appeared. "Now you're really in big—" he began as a dart hit him. *Splash!*

A third policeman appeared. "Now you're really in big—" he began as a dart hit him. *Splash!*

Then a fourth policeman appeared. "I'm new," he told her. Dubois fired her gun, but she was out of darts.

Back at the circus, it was showtime!

"Strike up the band!" Stefano shouted.

"You have a band?" Marty asked.

In response, a dog leaned on a boom box and pressed play.

"Prepare to be blown away!" Stefano told Alex.

"Blow me away!" Alex said, ready for the show.

"Here we go!" Stefano announced.

The animals hit the spotlights, and Stefano rolled out on a large ball, trying to juggle.

The Zoosters cheered.

"It's nice to be home!" Stefano called, still trying

to juggle. Then he slipped on the ball and fell down.

The Zoosters cheered, trying to encourage Stefano.

Stefano got back up on the ball and tried to juggle again. But the show was not going well. In fact, it was downright horrible!

The horses—Esmarelda, Ernstina, and Esperanza—trotted around the perimeter of the ring. In the midst of their display, one of the horses stopped in front of a pile of hay and started eating!

"Mystifying!" Stefano shouted, trying to divert the audience's attention from the horses.

Next, the dancing dogs came out. But in the middle of their dance, one of the dogs spotted his tail and started to chase it! Then another dog chased after a loose ball.

"Whoa! How do dogs do that?" Stefano said, trying to cover up the mistakes.

But the audience wasn't buying it; they were growing restless. "Get on with it!" they shouted.

Then it was Vitaly's turn. He walked up to the hoop, but instead of going *through* it, he walked *around* it! Smugly, he smacked his chest.

"Incredible!" Stefano shouted as the crowd booed.

Backstage, the Zoosters were growing concerned. This show was a flop!

The elephants were up next. They stood on rubber balls and held on to each other using their trunks. But as they were trying to keep their balance, a little girl in the audience shot a piece of popcorn at one of them. The elephants lost their grips on the balls and started to roll around the ring. Then *pop!* One of the balls burst under the elephant's weight. Shocked by the sound, one of the horses reared up, sending a dog named Jonesy, who was on his back, flying into the crowd.

"Oy, watch it, mate!" Jonesy said, throwing punches at an audience member. The other dogs ran into the audience and pulled Jonesy away.

Just then, an elephant backed into the crowd and knocked a little girl's drink out of her hands.

"Well, that was worth the price of admission," Skipper said as he watched the mayhem from the balcony.

Stefano was still trying to hold the show together.

"Oh, isn't it fun staying up late?" he asked as he started to juggle again.

Alex was horrified. Things had gone from bad to worse. He picked up a hook and pulled Stefano off the stage. "Stefano, you know 'blown away' means good," Alex said, referring to what Stefano had told him earlier.

"Don't worry, the big finale is coming up," Stefano told him. He hurried to center stage, where his horses were set up.

"Hey, give me a down beat," Stefano said to his one-dog band.

Stefano started to play his horns, but instead of music, a horrible noise came out of the instrument. Everyone covered his or her ears.

"Oh no, no, this is not happening," Alex said. He closed his eyes, and images of the Circus Master from whom they had bought the circus flooded his mind.

"'You have a deal, *mi amigo*,'" Alex remembered the Circus Master saying.

As Alex finally put it together that they had been ripped off—that they had made a rotten deal and had bought a rotten circus—Stefano was still out on stage trying to save the show. Finally, when the acts finished, the bleachers were empty.

"Yes! Go out and getta food and come back!" Stefano said, still not admitting that they were a total flop and that the crowd had left.

But the crowd had not left the scene of the circus totally. They were standing outside the ticket booth, demanding their money back!

Inside the booth, Mason and Phil were dressed as the ticket takers. They didn't know what to do with the crowd, so they scribbled down a sign and put it up.

BACK IN V, the sign read. But the people didn't want to wait five minutes for their money; they wanted it *now*!

Backstage, Alex was breathing into a paper bag. He was so upset at what was happening that he felt like he was going to faint!

"Deep breaths," Marty told him. "You're in a happy place, it's all good."

Just then, Phil and Mason rushed in. "There is an angry mob outside and they're demanding their money

84

back," Mason reported, pointing to the bag of money Phil was carrying.

"I think we all know the right thing to do," Skipper stated.

And what was that? *Get out of there fast!*

Luckily, Julien and Sonya had returned from their Roman adventure, so they could make the getaway, too. The Circus Train pulled out of town, and the animals ran to catch up. One by one, the animals hopped on the train as the angry crowd chased them.

"Come on, hurry up!" Marty urged Stefano, who was falling behind the train.

Stefano ran, still clutching his horns. He ran and ran and ran—then he dropped his horns! Stefano could not leave them behind; they were part of his act. He started to go back for his instruments, but the crowd crushed them underfoot. Now Stefano was really in trouble—the crowd was about to crush *him*.

But just when it looked as though it was curtains down for Stefano, Alex dashed back and saved him. They raced to the train, and Melman whisked them up to safety.

"*Grazi*, Alice!" Stefano said, smacking a kiss on Alex's cheek.

Now the Chimps were the only ones left on the ground.

"C'mon! Throw us the money! Hurry! They're gaining on you!" the Zoosters urged from inside the Circus Train.

The Chimps lobbed the moneybags into the air, but they didn't make it to the Zoosters. Instead, the bags exploded, and money rained down on the crowd. As the people scrambled for the cash, the Zoosters yanked Phil and Mason aboard.

"Aaack!" Julien cried as he watched his money disappear.

The money was gone, but at least they had escaped the hands of the angry mob. The animals settled into the car as the train chugged off into the night.

# CHAPTER 12

"This is a disaster," Alex said as he stared sadly out the barred windows of the train into the night. "We blew all our money on a bad circus."

"And we're not any closer to New York," Gloria put in.

"If anything, we're further away," Melman added.

Gloria and Melman were right. The train was chugging its way through the Alps—a long, long way from New York City.

"We could have at least bought a circus where they know how to circus!" Marty said.

Skipper, who was listening to this conversation, turned to the Penguins and said, "I don't even know why we bought a circus in the first place. We had enough dough for a plane."

"Are you kidding me?" Melman asked incredulously.

"You must have some money left over," Gloria said to Skipper.

Skipper grinned and held up a pair of golden dentures. "I used it to buy teeth," he told them. "And then had them capped in gold. Now I can eat apples. Sadly, I discovered I don't like apples."

Marty, Alex, Melman, and Gloria just shook their heads. Skipper was *unbelievable*! But they had to face the truth now—there was no way they were going to make it back home traveling with this circus.

"No promoter is sending this show to America; it's toe up!" Marty concluded.

Alex was distraught. He paced up and down the train car, trying to figure out what to do. Then, from out of nowhere, Stefano popped up in front of the window.

"Psst!" Stefano called to a startled Alex.

Gloria, Marty, and Melman didn't notice Stefano outside as they continued their conversation.

"Now it all makes sense," Gloria said. "No wonder the Circus Master was so happy to sell."

"He was happy, all right," Marty agreed, "happy about ripping us off."

Alex was curious about what Stefano wanted, so he opened the train door. *Whoosh!* A gust of wind pulled Alex outside. The door slammed shut, and Gloria, Marty, and Melman looked up.

"Where did Alex go?" Gloria asked.

"I dunno," Marty answered with a shrug.

What the others didn't know was that Alex was outside the train. And he was barely hanging on!

"Aaaagggh!" Alex cried as the train traveled on the edge of a cliff. Somehow, he managed to climb up to the top of the train. Once at the top, he saw Stefano a few cars away, leaping from one car to the next.

"Come on!" Stefano shouted to Alex. "This way!"

"No, no, no! You come this way!" Alex called out, beckoning him to come closer.

Stefano turned and waved. "Hey, Alice! Watcha your head!"

*Head?* Alex wondered. Then he turned to see that a tunnel was approaching—and fast!

Alex sprinted across the car. He turned back. The tunnel was gaining on him! In a few seconds he would be crushed! Frantically, he tried to run, but tripped. Thinking fast, Alex turned his blunder into a shoulder roll and was instantly on his feet again.

"Alice!" Stefano called out.

Just before impact, Alex did a handspring, leaped into the air, and flipped—all which carried him to the gap between the cars just as the lip of the tunnel blew overhead. *Phew!*

Alex tried to catch his breath as he hung upside down between the cars. The train barreled through the dark tunnel. Alex was momentarily startled as sparks came off the tracks, but he took comfort in the fact that he was safe. He shuddered at the thought of what could have been and then relaxed as the train exited the tunnel into the moonlit night.

A train door opened, and a worried Stefano appeared, holding a lantern. "Alice!" he called.

"I'm fine," Alex told him.

Stefano followed the sound of Alex's voice and saw him safely hanging by his claws between the train cars.

"Fantastic! Was that Trapeze Americano?" Stefano asked.

"Uh, yeah, sort of," Alex answered sarcastically.

"Incredible!" Stefano congratulated him.

"I hope this is important," Alex said, growing annoyed.

"Come this way, Alice," Stefano said, motioning to an open train car.

Alex retracted his claws and dropped down. Then he sprang off the railing and did a shoulder roll into the train car.

"By the way, it's -*icks*, not -*iss*. Alex. Like New York Knicks," Alex said, trying to explain to Stefano how to correctly pronounce his name.

"I know, New York Kniss," Stefano said. "Is not that hard."

Alex sighed.

Stefano followed Alex inside the train car and

turned on the lights. As the train car illuminated, Alex looked around the fancy room. Red velvet curtains hung on the windows, antique furniture sat on the floor, and the walls were covered with framed photos and posters from the circus's past.

"Whoa, what is this place?" Alex asked.

"I know you think we are stinky poopy circus," Stefano began, "but there is something you must know." Stefano turned on more lights and continued. "There was a time when Circus Zaragoza, we were a great circus. Numero uno in all of Europa." He turned on another light that illuminated a poster of Vitaly—a younger, happier Vitaly.

"And Vitaly—he was the biggest star of us all," Stefano told Alex. "He was fearless, taking risks, always new. He jumpa through the hoop like he could fly."

Stefano closed his eyes and remembered the good old days. He saw a young, slim, vibrant Vitaly flying through hoops. The crowd went wild.

"Stefano, make the hoop smaller," Vitaly the star had said.

"Like-a this?" Stefano had asked, twirling the mustache he had. He showed Vitaly a narrower hoop.

"Smaller," Vitaly requested.

Stefano dragged out an even narrower hoop—a hoop too narrow for the tiger to jump through. "Like this?" Stefano asked.

"Good." Vitaly was satisfied.

Vitaly popped open a bottle of olive oil and doused his body with it. Then he took a few steps back, drew in a deep breath, and raced toward the hoop.

*Swoosh!* Vitaly sailed through, and the crowd went wild!

Stefano momentarily snapped out of his daydream to explain to Alex: "It had never been done before because it was physically impossible. And the people, they loved it."

Stefano closed his eyes again and remembered the audience jumping to their feet. "Go, Vitaly!" they shouted.

Vitaly grabbed two bottles of oil, tossed them up in the air, then grabbed them again and poured the oil all over his body.

"Smaller!" Vitaly shouted.

Stefano produced an even narrower hoop, and Vitaly flew through that one, too! The crowd went crazy.

"And the hoop, she-a got smaller," Stefano explained to Alex. "Like the ring on the finger of the tiniest lady with the slimmest of fingers."

Stefano remembered how he brought out a very, very small hoop.

"Bravo, Vitaly!" the crowd shouted, encouraging him to make it through that one.

Vitaly grabbed an even bigger bottle of oil and poured it over his body.

"He would not stop pushing, and one fateful day, he pusha too far," Stefano explained.

Stefano shuddered as he recalled Vitaly standing in the center of the big top, sizing up a very narrow hoop.

"Light the hoop on fire!" Vitaly commanded as a gasp went through the crowd.

The hoop was lit on fire. The crowd sat on the edges of their seats and waited.

Vitaly grabbed a different bottle of olive oil—one

# MARTY

## THE    AMAZING

## ZEBRA

**LIVE BEFORE YOUR VERY EYES!**

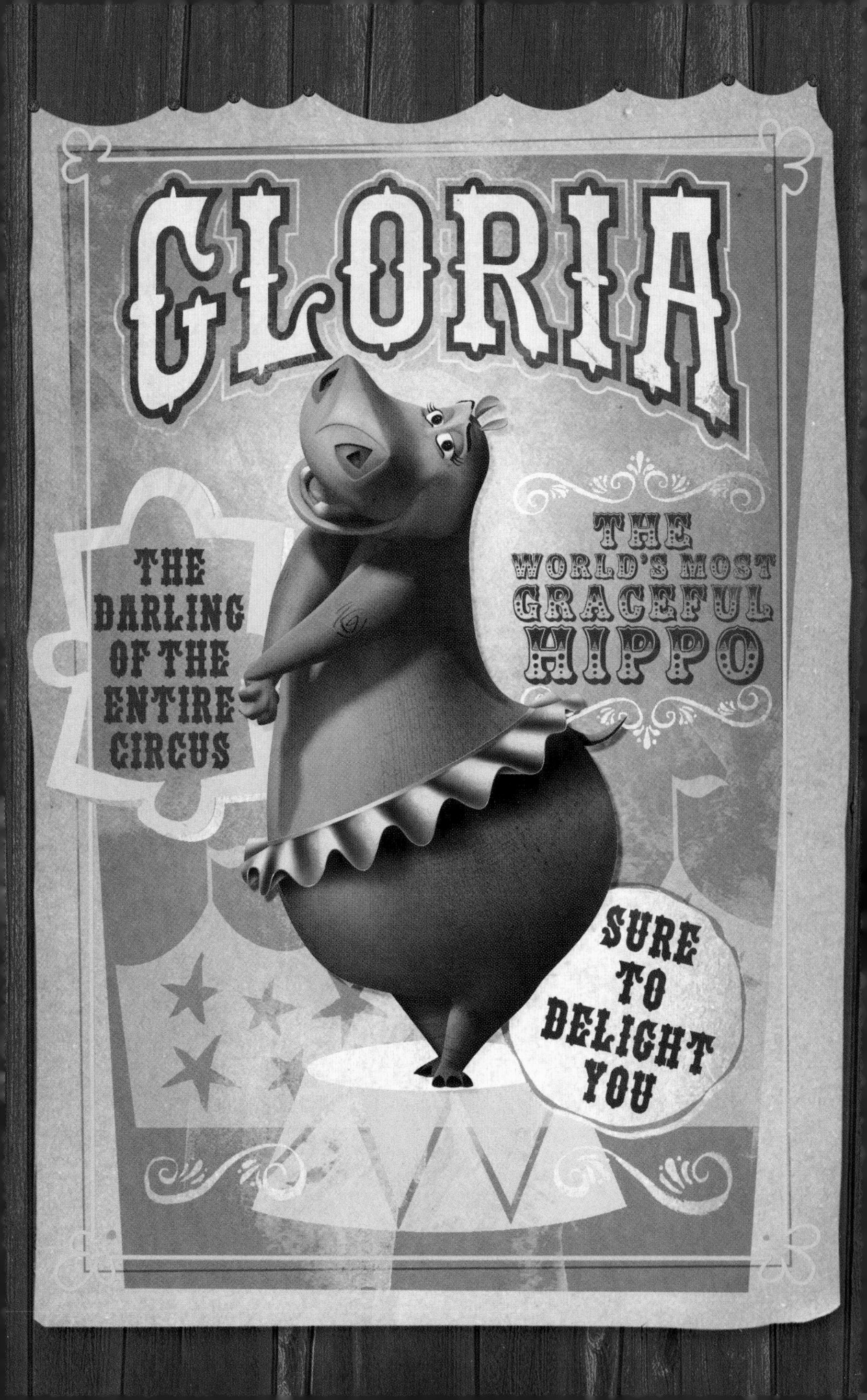
GLORIA
THE DARLING OF THE ENTIRE CIRCUS
THE WORLD'S MOST GRACEFUL HIPPO
SURE TO DELIGHT YOU

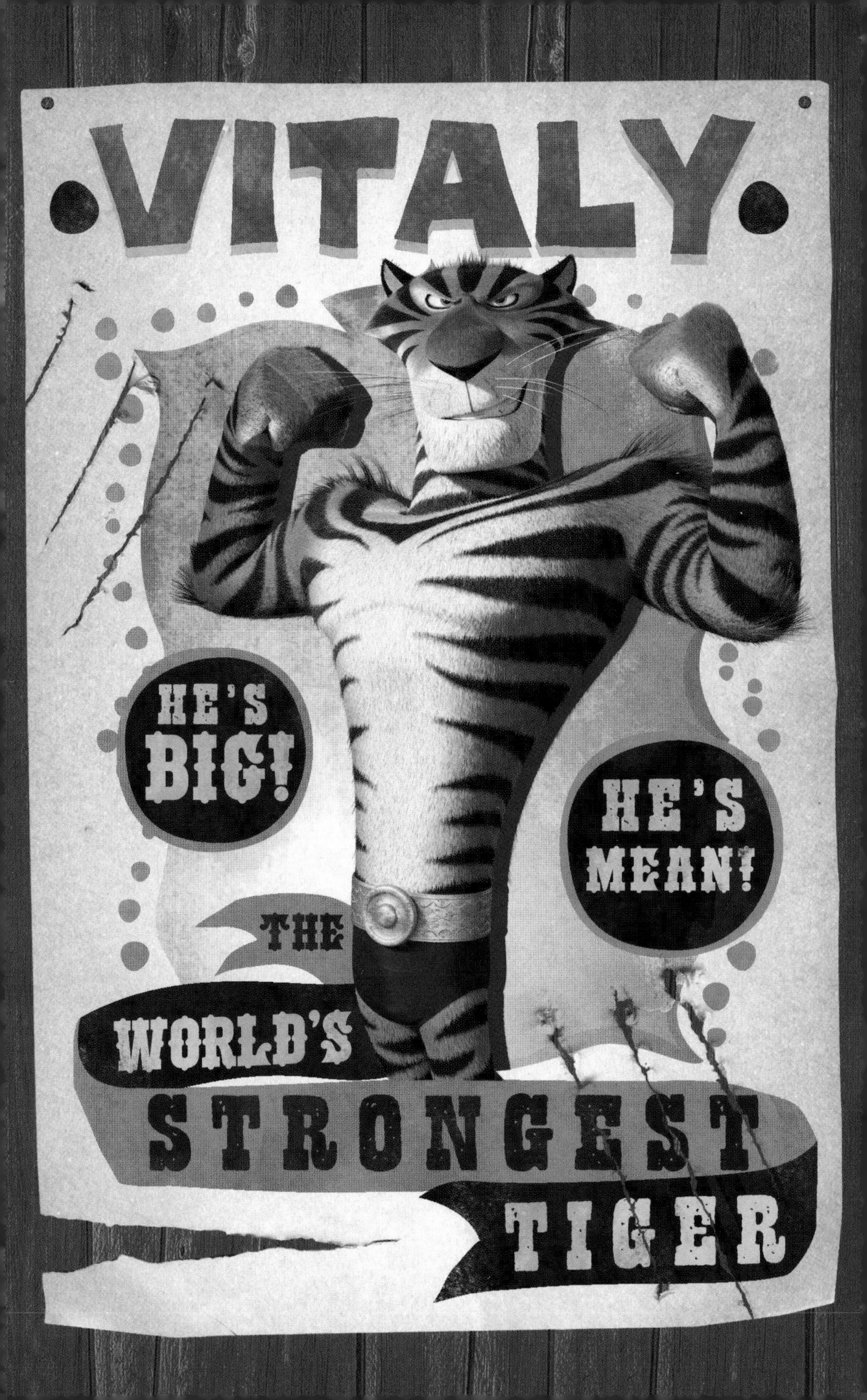
VITALY
HE'S BIG!
HE'S MEAN!
THE
WORLD'S
STRONGEST
TIGER

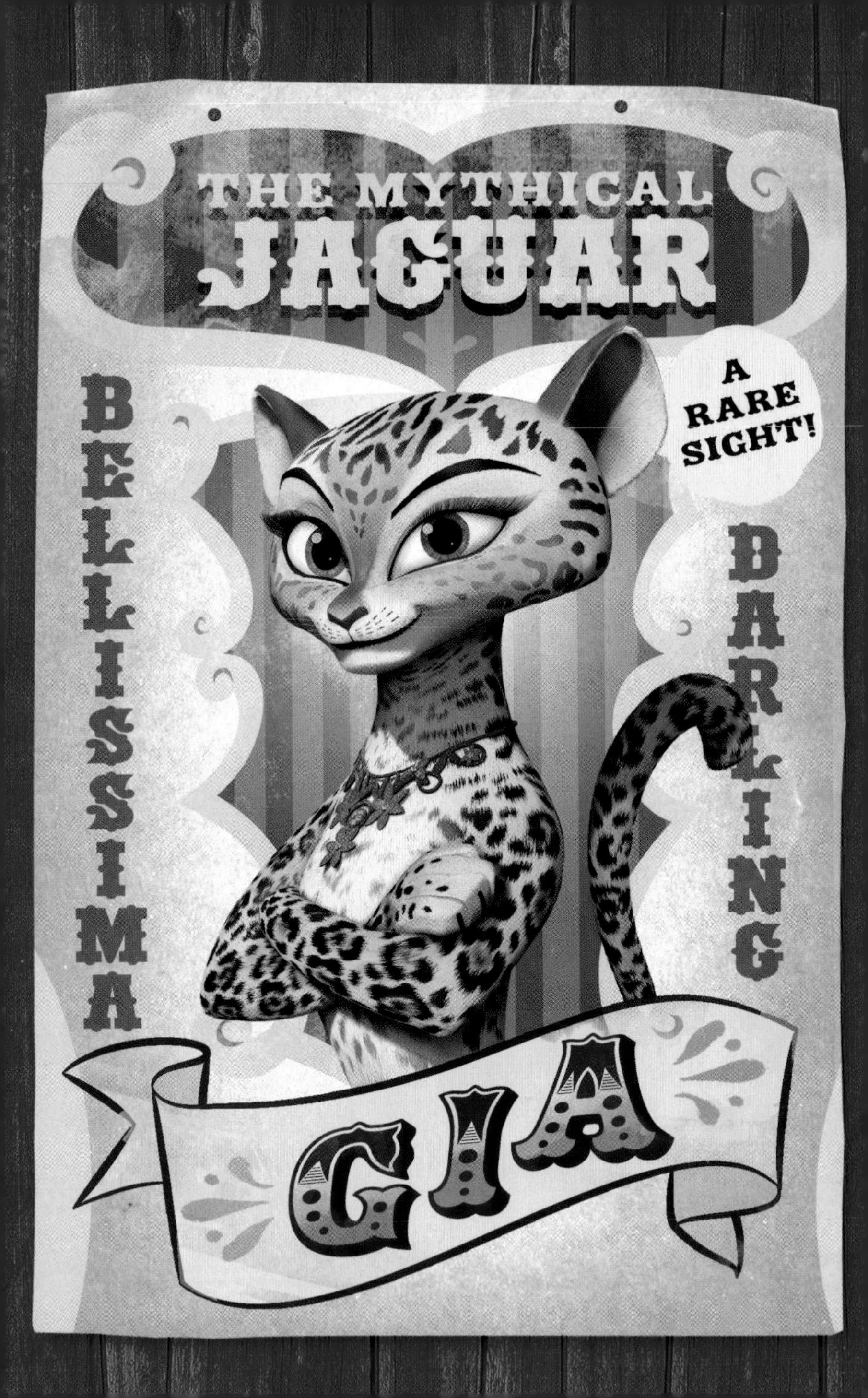
THE MYTHICAL
JAGUAR
A RARE SIGHT!
BELLISSIMA
DARLING
GIA

SENSATIONAL SONYA

THE BEAR

ONLY IN THE CIRCUS

A SHOWSTOPPING ACT

that read EXTRA VIRGIN. He poured the green oil all over his body, took a few steps back, and ran.

*Thunk!*

"Aaagh!" Vitaly screamed as he burst into flame.

Stefano grabbed a fire extinguisher and doused the flames.

"He fly too close to the sun and he got burned," Stefano told Alex. "Literally. The extra virgin olive oil is extra flammable."

Stefano continued his story. "And he-a lost everything. His wife—she ran off with a musician. He lost his dignity, his fame, his passion—and his fur. And when it-a grow back, it is less soft, more like a prickly beard. His only passion-a now is the borscht," Stefano said, referring to the soup Vitaly liked to eat.

"Whoa" was all Alex could say after he heard the story.

"He was our inspiration," Stefano told Alex. "So when he lost his passion, well, as Vitaly goes, so goes the circus. This is why we need your help."

"What sort of help?" Alex wanted to know.

"You can teach us to do new circus, Americano style," Stefano said brightly. "We find new passion, make new show, and we go all the way to *U S* and the *A*!"

Stefano jumped on a chair and slid past Alex, but he ended up facing the wrong way. Without missing a beat, he twisted and turned his body to get the chair to face Alex. After a few tries, he got the chair to face the right way and ended with a "ta-da" pose.

Alex looked at Stefano, lost in thought.

Stefano saw Alex's expression and was disappointed. "I know. It is stupido idea. We are a lost cause," Stefano said, turning off the desk lamp.

"No, no, no, this isn't stupido, this could work!" Alex told him.

Stefano turned the desk lamp back on. "What?"

"What you just said," Alex replied.

"What?" a confused Stefano asked again.

"The idea you just said, two seconds ago," Alex repeated.

"What?" Stefano asked, still not getting it.

"Your stupido idea," Alex said one more time.

"It could?" Stefano asked as it finally sank in.

Alex was really excited. "Stefano, you are a genius!"

"No, no, no. I'm only average intelligence," Stefano said modestly. "Some say I'm even slightly below."

"We are going to rethink everything anybody's ever known about a circus!" Alex said. "I call it Phase Four Dash Seven B, wherein in order to get home, we will come up with something fresh, something amazing, something brand-new! Fresh, never before seen, off the chain! Something that will blow the circus promoter away!"

Alex was supercharged. And who could blame him? He had found their ticket home!

# CHAPTER 13

Alex was very excited about his plan to reinvent the circus. He rushed to find the other circus animals to tell them about his idea. They were bound to like what he had to say, right?

Wrong!

"Forget it. You gotta be kidding me! Who does this guy think he is? You can't make us do that! What's he talking about? This is ridiculous! Change the circus? Is he crazy?" the circus animals protested.

Vitaly flung his knives at Alex. "I missed," he said as another knife landed in the wall behind Alex.

"Off with his head!" Julien said, joining the protest.

"C'mon, fellas! We can take him!" Jonesy threatened.

The train was stopped in an isolated Alpine clearing. Alex and the other Zoosters faced the circus animals. Vitaly stepped forward and confronted Alex.

"Circus been same for generations. We make good, classic family entertainment," he stated.

"Aha! But last few generations, families not so entertained," Stefano said, taking Alex's side. He didn't care what the circus animals thought; the circus *needed* a change!

"That's right," Alex spoke up. "Families not so entertained because you're just going through the motions out there. It's missing passion."

"How one to have passion for stool poked in face?" Vitaly wanted to know. Vitaly knew that it wasn't fun when the circus trainer poked and prodded the circus animals for the sake of an entertaining show.

"Exactly!" Marty said. "And by *stool* you mean *chair*, right?"

"The fact is, you guys got stuck in a rut," Alex said. "You stopped pushing. You stopped taking risks. But those days are over, because now we are going to

completely change the show."

"Then it wouldn't be a circus, would it?" a circus dog named Frankie stated.

"Circus is not about the acts you do. Circus is in here," Alex said as he touched the chest of Freddie, another circus dog.

Freddie looked down at the spot Alex had touched.

"How come Freddie gets all the circus?" Jonesy asked angrily.

The other dogs leaned over and looked at Freddie's chest, and Freddie lashed out and punched one of them!

"Circus is about following your passions wherever they take you," Alex continued.

"You cannot change circus," Vitaly repeated. "There is long tradition."

"That's what everybody thought, Vitaly—until those French Canadians came along, drunk off their maple syrup and cheap pharmaceuticals, and completely flipped the paradigm," Alex said, describing another circus act.

"Now they play Vegas!" Marty added, emphasizing

how big that act got. "Fifty shows a day. In fifty-two separate venues!"

"And you know *how* they did it?" Alex asked. "They got rid of the animals!"

"Say it ain't so!" Marty cried.

The other animals gasped in horror. No animals in a circus? How could that possibly be?

"Well, you know what I say to that?" Alex asked. "I say, they can take the animals out of the circus, but they *cannot* take the animals out of the circus!" Alex continued.

The animals stared at him. What was he talking about?

"I mean, they cannot—err," Alex stuttered. "I think you understand what I'm saying!"

The animals got it and started to rally around him.

"Yes!" Stefano shouted.

"Ah, no!" Julien disagreed.

"We don't need humans! Because we've got passion," Alex continued his pep talk. "What does a human say when he's passionate? He says, 'I'm an animal!' Well, we *are* animals! We'll make an all-animal circus. Because if we follow our passions, we can go anywhere!"

"Anywhere!" Marty said, popping up between the dogs.

Alex leaped onto a nearby pedestal. "We can do anything!" he shouted.

"Anything!" Marty repeated, popping up next to Gloria.

"If we do it together," Alex concluded.

"All of us!" Marty cheered, popping up next to Alex.

Now all the animals cheered. Even the dogs were ready to join in.

"Yes! We're in!" Jonesy said. "We'll have some of that! Oy!"

"Can I hear you say 'fur power'? Fur power!!" Marty shouted.

"Fur power!! Fur power!!" the animals joined in.

Gloria was excited, too. She turned to Melman and said, "You and me, baby! An act together!"

"I love it!" Melman agreed.

"We can do that funkengrooven dance thing!" Gloria told him.

Melman hesitated. "Uh, dance?"

"This thing right here, look," Gloria said as she started to dance. "Me and you. We got this."

Melman whimpered. "Yeah, but I can't dance."

As Gloria tried to get Melman to dance, the other animals excitedly started to reinvent themselves. They had lots of ideas for new circus acts.

Gia was excited, too. "Fur power! Fur power!" she shouted.

"Chanting is fun!" Stefano agreed. "Chanting is fun! Chanting is fun!"

Just then, Vitaly slammed his battle-axe into the ground. "I do not trust this lion. He has his own circus. What does he want with ours?"

"Vitaly, I may not trust him, either, but I am tired of sitting and standing and rolling over," Gia said, referring to her boring circus act.

"There is great tradition of sitting, standing, rolling over," Vitaly said proudly.

"You know our circus is in trouble," Gia reasoned. "This could be our last chance. But we will not do this without you."

"Circus always stay together," Stefano put in.

Vitaly thought about what Gia and Stefano said. "Okay, I do the hoop," he finally agreed.

Gia was so happy that she hugged Vitaly.

"I want to hug, too!" Stefano said.

Vitaly and Gia hugged their friend.

And there, on Vitaly's face, was something that no one had seen in a long, long time—a smile.

# CHAPTER 14

The animals decided the Alpine clearing was the perfect place to practice. If you looked up, you could see the sun bouncing off the Alps' peaks. And if you looked down, you would see the animals as they rehearsed their new acts—bouncing and rolling, hopping and swinging.

"More boom sticks, Rico! I really want to fly!" Stefano ordered.

"Are you really going to shoot yourself out of that thing?" Marty asked, pointing to the cannon that Stefano stood on top of.

Stefano put on a crash helmet, climbed to the muzzle of the cannon, and slipped inside. Rico tossed a ton of dynamite into the muzzle.

"I've always dreamed of doing this—from-a the time I was a leetle pup," Stefano told Marty and the Penguins. "To be human cannonball—except, you know, a *sea lion* cannonball."

"Is it dangerous?" Marty asked.

"Is it dangerous?" Stefano repeated. "Yes! Of course it's dangerous!" But Stefano didn't sound scared, he sounded *excited*.

Rico shoved the last stick of dynamite into Stefano's mouth and jumped down.

"Are you sure about this?" Marty asked as the cannon barrel rose.

"I am sure," Stefano said. "Really sure!"

"Because if blowing up is your thing, then you're in the right place!" Marty exclaimed.

"*Sì!*" Stefano answered. "That means *yes*."

The barrel locked into firing position.

"Ready for launch?" Skipper asked.

"Ready for launch," Stefano agreed.

Kowalski lit the fuse, and Skipper said, "Fire in the hole!"

"Wait!" Stefano said, spitting out the dynamite. He was losing his nerve, but it was too late.

*Blam!* Stefano was launched into the air. But Rico used too much dynamite, and Stefano flew over the inflatable target—*way* over.

*"Aaaagh! Ooof!"* Stefano exclaimed as he slammed into a cliff. "Mamma mia! Help me!" he shouted, hanging on to the cliff with all his might. One little slip and that would be it!

"Rico! Get the cannon ready! Same charge!" Marty commanded, springing into action.

Moments later, the muzzle of the cannon rose. Marty was inside, ready to be launched.

"Fire in the hole!" Skipper shouted.

*Blam!* Marty flew through the air. But instead of being terrified like Stefano, Marty was thrilled. He stuck out his legs like the wings on a fire jet. A huge smile spread across his face—he was flying!

"All right! Oooh yeah!" Marty barrel-rolled past a double rainbow. He flew through the clouds, then— *smack!*—he plowed into the cliff just above Stefano.

"Marty, I'm so glad you're here!" Stefano said.

"Woo!! I was flying!" Marty said, still excited.

"Yes, I am proud of you, but I don't think I can hold on much longer," Stefano struggled to say.

Marty got back to business. "Right! Sorry about my enthusiasm!" He jammed his hoof into a crack in the rock and hung upside down. "Here! Wrap this around you!" he said, tossing the looped end of a rope to Stefano.

Stefano quickly wrapped the rope around his body. But then he slipped! Luckily, Marty was holding on to the other end of the rope and saved him.

*"Agh!"* Stefano cried as he dangled in the air.

"All right, I got ya!" Marty assured him.

Marty worked the rope through his hooves and teeth and lowered Stefano. Finally Stefano landed safely on the ground, and Marty rappelled down behind him.

"Forget about being part of the herd," Marty said once he was back on the ground, too. "I'm gonna be part of the flock! I'm gonna fly, baby!"

"Oh yes, what a triumph!" Stefano said.

A new act for the circus was born!

# CHAPTER 15

Now that Marty had his act, Gloria and Melman needed theirs. Gloria was still intent on dancing. She pushed the button on the circus boom box and dance music played. Gloria hummed to the music as she stretched her muscles.

"Hey, Gloria!" Melman shouted. "Instead of the funkinblahblah dance thing, I was thinking . . ." He whipped out a bunch of bowling pins. "Ta-da!" he shouted.

"Bowling?" Gloria asked, regarding the pins.

"No, no. Juggling," he said as he started to juggle. Or *tried* to juggle.

"Look! Watch, watch. Here we go! Here we go!"

Melman dropped the pins. "Okay, okay, forget about juggling. Oh! I know!" Melman said, desperately looking around for another idea. Then he spotted the high wire. "Tightrope!" he announced.

"What about your acrophobia?" Gloria asked him, meaning his fear of heights.

"Oh, so what, you don't think I can do the tightrope?" Melman asked with a scowl. "Is that it?"

"I just thought we could dance together," Gloria told him. "It would be exciting!"

"You know, just forget it," Melman replied.

"Melman," Gloria urged. She didn't want Melman to give up.

"I'm gonna do my own thing," Melman said. And with that, he walked away.

In another part of the clearing, Skipper was overseeing the working Penguins and Chimps. Rico had just finished cutting and stacking a pile of wood.

"Well, that's a dozen less spotted owls to worry about!" Skipper commented, regarding the felled trees. "Who needs a lumberyard?"

A few feet away, the Chimps were busy hammering boards.

"Splendid!" Mason observed as he hammered in a nail. Then *bang!* He hammered a nail into Phil's thumb. Oops! Ouch!

While the Chimps were busy hammering, Mort and Maurice were busy sawing. Mort stood on top of a log that Maurice pushed toward a saw. The log rolled closer and closer to the saw. Mort watched as the dust flew. What was Mort doing? In another second, he'd be turned into sawdust, too! At the last moment, Mort jumped from the log, just as it was sawed in half.

Meanwhile, Alex was trying to break up a dogfight.

"Hand over that circus, Freddie!" Jonesy said. He was still dwelling on the idea that Alex said the circus was inside the dog!

"No! It's mine!" Freddie said, still believing that he really had the circus.

"Hey, hey, hey," Alex cut in. "Put your weapons down. Guys, come on, chill out. Cute and cuddly is obviously not your thing."

"Oh, he's got us pegged," the dogs responded.

"I got a better idea," Alex told them. "Show 'em!"

Kowalski went over to Jonesy and strapped a pair of rocket-powered skates onto his back paws. Then Kowalski lit a fuse and started to count down.

*Whoosh!* Before Kowalski could announce "Blast off!" the skates fired and Jonesy shot off.

"Yaaiiii!" Jonesy cried as he flew like a rocket.

Then *boom!* Jonesy smashed into the side of a train car. Considering Jonesy's temper, the other animals thought that he'd be furious. But no—he was *happy*! Excited, even.

"Oh, that was great!" Jonesy said with a smile. "I like it!"

The skates fired again, and Jonesy was launched up into the air.

"Rocket shoes! I want to try that!" each dog cried.

Just then, Gia walked up.

"Hey, hi . . . ," Alex said nervously.

"I admire how you have inspired these animals," Gia complimented him.

"Oh, thanks," Alex responded.

"And what you said about passion. It was like poetry," Gia continued.

"I love passion and poetry; they go together, really. I mean, I know they don't rhyme," Alex rambled.

"Trapeze is my passion," Gia told Alex.

"Terrific. I look forward to seeing you up there on the—"

"You can teach me," Gia interrupted.

*Oh no*, Alex thought. He didn't know the first thing about trapeze. Quickly, he started to walk away. But he just couldn't leave her standing there; he had to think of something to say.

"Oh, well, you know, I've always been kind of a solo act," he managed. "So that kind of rules that out."

"I wonder if you actually do trapeze," Gia challenged.

"Oh, I actually do trapeze," Alex told her.

"Show me," Gia stated.

"'Show me'?" Alex mimicked. "What are we, five?"

"I am five, yes," Gia told him. "Show me."

Alex sighed. There was nothing more to say. Gia had won. But how in the world was he going to teach her something he didn't know the first thing about?

# CHAPTER 16

While Alex tried to figure out how to teach Gia the trapeze, Melman tried to figure out how to walk the tightrope. (And get over his fear of heights!)

Melman climbed a ladder that led up to the high wire. "Psshht, dancing. All you're doing is moving and not getting anywhere," he muttered to himself as he climbed. "I mean, the music totally throws off my timing. You want excitement? Check it out. Who's on a tightrope? Huh? Who's on a tightrope?"

Suddenly, Melman realized that *he* was the one on the tightrope! "Ahhh! I'm on a tightrope. I'm on a tightrope! Help me!" The more Melman panicked, the more the wire shook. Melman struggled to keep his balance.

Just then, Gloria appeared. "Melman! Oh my gosh! Baby, hold on!" she shouted. "Don't move. Just hold on, sweetie. I'm gonna get you down. Hold on, baby, I'm coming! Stay right there."

Frantically, Gloria climbed the ladder. But just as she reached the platform, Melman fell! Luckily, he grabbed the rope with his chin, spun around, and landed on top of the wire.

"Melman! Baby, hold on," Gloria shouted again. "Just calm down, Melman."

Carefully, Gloria slid out on the tightrope.

Melman tried to look up to see where Gloria was, but when he did, he started to shake uncontrollably. "Ahhh! I'm gonna f-fall!" Melman cried.

Gloria tried to hang on to the shaky tightrope. At the same time, she tried to reassure Melman that he was not going to fall.

But Melman was still terrified. "I'm gonna fall and break all of my neck!" he said.

Slowly, Gloria inched her way across. But she was so heavy that the wire started to sag. Down below, the elephants pulled on the rope that secured the tightrope to the ground. The wire tightened.

"I promise you," Gloria said in a shaky voice. "Just look at me. Look at me! All eyes on me."

Melman looked up and saw Gloria and momentarily regained his balance. "Okay," he agreed.

"Come to me," Gloria told him.

"I can't," Melman responded.

"It's just like dancing," Gloria explained. "Two steps forward. One step back."

Melman started to shake. "I can't dance, okay! There, I said it."

"Maybe because you've never tried," Gloria told him.

"No, I have tried!" Melman shot back. "I practiced in private because you dance so well! And so I tried, but I can't. Now you know!"

Gloria was shocked. "You practiced? For me?"

As they talked, they glided closer together.

"Yes," Melman said, admitting that he practiced just for Gloria. "But it's no use. I never know what to do with my arms!"

Just then, Melman misstepped! "Whoa!" he shouted.

Instantly, Gloria reached out and caught him. "Whoa, hold it, okay? That part's so easy, Melman, because all you have to do is put them around your partner. See?" And with that, Gloria guided Melman's arms around her neck. Melman smiled.

"Two steps forward. One step back," Gloria demonstrated. "Two steps forward, one step back."

"Hey, I'm dancing!" Melman said to Gloria. Then, calling to the elephants on the ground, he said, "We're dancing on the tightrope! Woo-hoo! I'm dancing!"

"You're great!" Gloria told him.

Then, almost as in celebration, a cannon blast rang out. And there, sailing through the air, was Stefano!

Now that more acts were finished, it was time for Gia to perfect her trapeze act—with Alex's help. Gia and Alex climbed up to the trapeze platform to start.

"Okay, all right," Alex said, stalling for time.

"We need the jet packs and aquatic cobras, no?" Gia said, remembering how Alex had described his trapeze act.

"Yes, but that's a pretty advanced maneuver," Alex fibbed. "This is a beginner's class."

"So how do we begin?" Gia wanted to know.

"Okay, well, it's a bit complicated unless you understand the whole pitch and yaw, arc and gravity," Alex said, still stalling. "All that stuff, which I won't bore you with. Okay . . ."

"You need a push?" Gia interrupted.

"No!" Alex exclaimed. "Just watch and learn—"

But he didn't get to finish his sentence because Gia pushed him off the platform! Down, down he fell, and luckily caught the hanging bar with his feet. Then he swung until he reached the other platform. But instead of landing gracefully, he caught the platform with his teeth!

Gia, on the other hand, was a graceful sight to behold. She flipped and somersaulted in the air. But her landing was less than graceful, as she, too, caught the platform with her teeth.

"Like that?" Gia asked through her clenched teeth.

"That's one way of doing it," Alex answered, also

through clenched teeth. But then he couldn't hold on any longer and fell. He hit his head on the bar, plummeted down to the net, and then popped back up onto the bar.

"Wow! You use the net!" Gia commented.

"Yes!" Alex agreed. "Trapeze Americano. We use the net."

Then Gia did the same thing—only better! "Trapeze Americano!" she exclaimed.

Alex took off for another move. He swung on the bar, hit the wooden pole, fell onto the net, and bounced back up. Gia did the same.

The horses stopped to watch as Alex and Gia performed more tricks. Then the dogs stopped to watch the show, too.

Alex went for another move, but missed the bar. But before he hit the net, Gia swung in, grabbed him, and they landed together on the platform.

"Wow!" Gia said breathlessly as she stared into Alex's eyes.

Then *wham!* Marty flew in from his cannon and

knocked them off the platform into the net. The three laughed as the rest of the animals cheered—except for Vitaly.

Alex stood up at the edge of the net and said, "Well, guys, I'd say we all found our acts."

Stefano noticed that everyone was cheering—except for Vitaly. Maybe he needed an extra push. Stefano had known Vitaly when he was excited about the circus; maybe Stefano could help him get back to that state. "Hey, Vitaly, maybe you even do two hoop, huh?" Stefano asked.

Vitaly seemed to agree, but inside he was scared stiff!

The animals were ready to hit the road. The Chimps put the finishing touches on the train engine, and Skipper ordered everyone aboard.

"Grab your luggage and drain your bladders," he told them. "It's going to be a long ride."

Alex held out his hand for Gia and pulled her into one of the train cars. "All right, everybody," Alex announced. "Next stop, London! Let's blow that promoter away!"

Everyone cheered—everyone except for Vitaly.

Vitaly slid open the door to his car and opened a cabinet. Inside the cabinet were hoops—big hoops, small hoops, fat hoops, and thin hoops. Vitaly's eyes blazed as he imagined the hoops glowing with fire. Shuddering, he slammed the cabinet shut. There was no way he could re-create his act. His nerve was gone.

What was the great Vitaly going to do?

# CHAPTER 17

The Circus Train chugged its way to London. Once there, the animals set up the big top on the banks of the River Thames. Big Ben and the Westminster Bridge loomed in the background.

The people of London were excited to see the circus. They streamed into the tent and packed the house. Although the animals were excited that so many people had come out to see them, there was only one person they wanted there—the circus promoter.

"Come on, come on. Where is he?" Skipper asked as he scanned the crowd through a pair of binoculars.

Just then, the lenses landed on a large cowboy hat. The man wearing it had a bald eagle perched on his shoulder. That had to be him—the lone American in the crowd.

"Bingo," Skipper said. "If that's not a red-blooded American promoter, I don't know what is."

Everyone was ready and waiting backstage. The Penguins were dressed in top hats and bow ties, and Alex was checking out the crowd.

"We need to get this show on the road," Skipper said, passing his binoculars to Alex. "Private, tell them the eagle has landed."

"The eagle has landed," Private repeated.

"Roger that!" Alex said in response to Skipper's coded message. He went through his last-minute checklist.

"We're on, folks!" Alex shouted as he walked excitedly through the backstage area. "All right, guys, let's go!"

The horses walked up to Alex, and one of them asked, "Do we go on before or after the dogs?"

"Yes," Alex replied.

"What?" the horse named Esmarelda asked, confused.

124

"Overlap," Alex clarified. "Your acts overlap."

Then Alex walked over to where Marty, Melman, and Gloria were warming up. "Hey, guys, guess what? The promoter is in the house!" he told them.

"New York is closer than ever!" Marty exclaimed.

"Ooh! I'm so excited!" Gloria put in.

The Zoosters were sure that the circus promoter would love their show so much that he'd sign them to a US tour—which would stop in New York, of course.

"I don't want to jinx it, but I don't think I care, because I think we just might actually pull this off," Alex said giddily. "All right, animals!" he called out. "Let's go! This is it. Showtime!"

And what a show it was. Everything fell perfectly into place. The Chimps played their colorful organ. The dogs flew through the ring on their rocket-powered skates. Sonya rode around on her new motorcycle. Vitaly flew through the hoop, Gloria and Melman danced on the high wire, and Alex and Gia did their trapeze act. The cannon act was amazing—the audience leaped to their feet when Marty and Stefano were shot in the air. *Oohs* and *ahh*s could be heard coming from the crowd when the elephants swung on their silk rope while spraying fire through their trunks and the horses bounced on trampolines with butterfly wings on their backs.

The audience was thrilled, and so were the animals. The circus was a hit! In fact, the circus was such a hit that the circus promoter walked backstage with a contract in his hand! The Chimps, dressed as the Circus Master, accepted a pen from the promoter's pet eagle and inked the deal.

"We're going to America, everybody!" Alex told all the animals after the show.

"We did it! Yeah! Fur power! We were amazing!" the animals shouted with joy.

"Now *that's* what I call a crack-a-ackin to the mack-a-lackin!" Marty shouted.

"We did it, Alice!" Stefano exclaimed.

"Yeah!" Alex agreed.

Stefano was pleased. "Maybe I am average intelligence after all!" he said.

"Perhaps even slightly above," Alex said with a smile.

Gia grabbed Alex and hugged him. "Wow! Gia and Alex, the Trapezing Cats."

"We did pretty good," Alex acknowledged.

"You will flip and I will catch," Gia told Alex. "And sometimes, I will flip and you will catch, and then we will travel the whole world. Flipping and catching . . ."

Alex listened to Gia, trying to figure out what she was talking about. Suddenly, he got it—she was asking him to stay.

Gia looked hopefully into Alex's eyes.

"You know, the thing is, I think you should maybe plan on doing the trapeze by yourself," Alex told her.

"By myself?" Gia questioned.

"Yeah, I mean, I might not always be around," Alex told her.

"Where are you going?" Gia wanted to know.

"Well, I-I-I . . . we'll be going back to our own circus," Alex stammered.

"Oh, of course," Gia said, disappointed.

"That's Bolshevik," Vitaly interjected. "I am sorry,

Gia, but they are leaving to go back to their *zoo*."

The circus animals all let out a shocked gasp.

Gia, too, was stunned. "*Zoo?* You are from a zoo?"

"Yes," Alex admitted, "but there's more."

"More?" Gia asked. What more could there be? A zoo was a zoo.

"They were never circus," Vitaly stated.

"We had to say we were circus," Melman put in.

"If we didn't, you would have never let us get on the train," Gloria added.

"Yes, and they use us to get back home," Vitaly said smugly.

"No, no, no," Alex protested. Then he admitted, "I mean, yes, but no."

"And Trapeze Americano?" Gia asked.

"It didn't exactly exist when I taught it to you, but—"

"I did something that does not exist?!" Gia interrupted.

"It exists *now!*" Alex told her.

Gia couldn't believe it—it was all a lie! "Jet packs and aquatic cobras," she said, shaking her head. Then she laughed. "Ha, I should have known."

"Balloons to the children of the world was not real, either?" Stefano wanted to know.

"Well, yeah, that's not real," Alex said. "But look at what I did!" Alex knew that he had lied, but he had helped create the circus—a new circus that was great! He should at least get some credit for that, right?

"I was shot out of a cannon. I could have died," Stefano said. He realized how much danger he had been in. He thought he was in the hands of professionals, but these animals were just posers—and users!

"But I thought it was your lifelong dream," Marty told Stefano.

Gia turned to Alex and said, "We trusted you."

Ouch!

"For all I know, your name is not really Alice," Stefano said.

Alex was defeated. "No, Stefano, but it never really was."

Stefano turned away from Alex and looked at Gia.

"Gia . . . ," Alex implored. She *had* to understand;

she *had* to forgive him. They had become friends—and partners—after all. But Gia did not give Alex a response. The only thing she gave him was an icy stare.

"My tears are real," Stefano told Alex. "You are not." And with that, he and Gia walked away.

The circus animals weren't going to let the Zoosters' lies stop them. They weren't going to miss the opportunity to perform in New York City. The circus animals boarded a ship headed for America. But the Zoosters weren't about to be left behind—this was their ticket back home. So they all piled into a small rowboat that was attached to the ship and started their journey across the sea.

The animals might have left London, but someone was still on their trail: Captain Chantel Dubois!

The crafty captain escaped prison and found her injured men recovering in the local hospital. But there was no time to spend lounging around in a hospital—they had a lion to catch!

Dubois tried to convince the men to join her, but they just complained about their aches and pains.

Suddenly, Dubois started to sing, and the men started to smile. *Voila!* They were better.

Quickly, Dubois got them out of bed and ready for action. Dubois and her men raced into town, searching for clues.

"I'm afraid we missed them," one of Dubois's men said as they stood around a poster.

"There, there, Gerard," Dubois comforted, petting Gerard's head. Then she flung a dog treat into his mouth!

Dubois walked up to the poster and read NEXT PERFORMANCE NEW YORK CITY. So the circus was on the road. "Our little kitty just wants to go home," Dubois said, pretending to care about Alex.

"But madam," another one of her men interjected. "If they get back to the zoo, the big game will be over."

"Not if we play by the rules of murder!" Dubois said, an evil gleam in her eye.

"Ah, which means, madam?"

"We get there first," she told him.

And with that, Dubois pulled out her dart gun and

spun it around. Suddenly, Gerard fell over. A dart was stuck in his back!

"Get up, Gerard," Dubois ordered.

Captain Chantel Dubois had a job to complete.

CHAPTER 18

The animals arrived in New York and set up the big top.

"Tomorrow, we will introduce the New Yorkers to their new king!" Julien said as he sat in Sonya's car. He looked in the mirror, adjusted his hat, and added, "and queen!"

"Bwwahh," Sonya responded.

"You know, that is a real turn-on," Julien said as Sonya chewed on a tire.

"Bwwahh," Sonya said again.

"Me? Stay with the circus?" Julien asked, understanding what Sonya had said. "I am a king. I don't think you realize a lemur of my status and

intellect and beauty and intellect . . . did I say intellect?"

Sonya grabbed him and began to wrestle.

"No, no time for friskiness," Julien said, trying to push her away. "I want to talk. No! You're squashing me! Stop it! No means no! Or in your language, *Arrrrwwill*!" Julien shouted as he pulled away.

*"Auunnnnggg!"* Sonya shouted in response.

"Not everything is solved that way, you know," Julien told her. He did not like how roughly Sonya was playing. On second thought, was that really playing?

Sonya stared blankly at Julien and walked away.

Julien was annoyed. "Sonya?! Are you listening to me?"

In response, Sonya climbed on top of a red ball.

"Now I'm getting the silent treatment, am I?" Julien asked as he walked over to Sonya. "Come over here right now! Don't shut me out, baby! What is wrong with you? *Speak!*"

*"Roar!"* Sonya answered.

"Okay! If these are your feelings, I understand now!" Julien told her. "I'm going." He headed for the door. "It's obvious I'm just an emotional whoopee cushion for you to sit on," he continued. "When you look for where I am, I won't be there!"

Then, with a sniffle and a wipe of a tear, Julien was gone.

This time, Sonya didn't fight or roar. This time, Sonya the bear was truly sad.

While the circus animals were preparing for the circus, the Zoosters were preparing to go back home.

"Well, we're here," Gloria said as she, Marty, Melman, Alex, and Julien stood outside the gates of the zoo.

"Wow!" Melman commented.

"My rock looks much smaller than I remember it," Alex observed.

"Look at the mural," Marty said, pointing to the painted African scenery. "Doesn't actually capture the real thing, does it?"

"Wow. I forgot about that wall in between us, Melman. Was that always there?" Gloria asked.

The Zoosters had forgotten a lot. They had spent

so much time as free animals in the wild that the zoo looked downright confining!

"Guys. I'm sorry I left the zoo in the first place," Marty told his friends. He was talking about how he had longed to see the outside world. His desire had been so strong that on his birthday a few years ago he actually left the zoo. Melman, Alex, and Gloria went after him to bring him home, but they never made it back to the zoo. Instead, they had wild adventures through Africa and Europe. "I mean, if I just stayed put, you wouldn't have anything to be sad about right now," Marty continued.

"You know, Marty," Alex said as he took a step back from the gate, "leaving the zoo was the best thing you could have done." It was all starting to make sense to Alex now. They *needed* to leave the zoo. Otherwise, they wouldn't have seen and done so much.

"Really?" Marty asked, surprised.

"Look what we did out there in the world. We saved the Lemurs from the dreaded foosa!" Alex told him.

"Thanks to my excellent plan," Julien put in.

Gloria started to feel a bit woozy. She turned to Melman and said, "We fell in love."

Melman, who felt woozy, too, said, "It took an African volcano to bring us together."

"I ran with the herd," Marty said woozily.

"I got to meet the parents I never knew I had," Alex added.

"You're not gonna find that in a zoo," Marty concluded.

And then Alex remembered their latest adventure. "We put on the most amazing circus the world has ever seen."

Just then, Alex heard a popping sound and his shoulder was thrust forward. "We were already home," Alex said, feeling very woozy.

"Sonya, baby!" Julien shouted. "I don't wanna be king." He stumbled into a nearby bush.

What was wrong with the Zoosters? If you looked closely at Julien, you could see that he had a dart sticking out of his forehead. A tranquilizer gun had shot him and the rest of the Zoosters!

"Let's run away with the circus," Marty declared.

"Wh-what?" Alex stuttered.

"We apologize. They t-take us back. Easy p-peasy," Marty said.

"I think it's t-too l-late," Alex said, his head spinning.

"Then we gr-grovel," Gloria suggested.

"I'm an excellent groveler," Melman put in.

The Zoosters blinked their eyes. Everything around them was spinning. What was going on?

"Hey, if groveling doesn't work, we own their little fuzzy butts," Marty said. He remembered that they still owned the circus! But that was the last thing he remembered before he fell to the ground, fast asleep.

And as soon as Marty passed out, so did Melman, Gloria, and Alex. They were all knocked out by Captain Dubois's darts!

Dubois knelt next to a sleeping Alex. "My prize, my delicate prize," she cooed. "He is so cute when he's sleeping; he almost looks dead."

"Madam! He will never fit in the carry-on,"

Gerard commented, wondering how they would get Alex back to Monte Carlo with them.

"We'll mount him right here, Gerard," Dubois said.

Aha! So *that* was her plan. Dubois was going to kill and stuff Alex. Then she'd bring the lion home as her prize. How horrid!

Dubois's men quickly pulled supplies from a duffel bag. Lastly, they took out a plaque that read LION—a plaque that was the perfect size for Alex's head.

Poor Alex. *Wake up!*

Just then, Dubois heard a man's voice. "Look what she's done!" the man exclaimed.

Dubois looked up and saw a group of uniformed men and women approaching. Innocently, she looked up and said, *"Quoi?"* (That means *what* in French.)

Dubois was so close—she had her prize in her hand. What was she going to do now?

*Quoi?*

# CHAPTER 19

The Fur Power big top was all set up. The animals were getting ready backstage when Julien came running in.

"Sonya! Sonya!" he cried, crashing into a crate. "Excuse me," he told the crate. Poor Julien was so groggy from the dart that he didn't know who—or what—he was talking to!

Julien staggered around backstage shouting and crying. "Sonyaaa! Where are you, Sonnnyyya?"

Just then, Sonya let out a loud roar.

"Sonya! Baby!" Julien shouted as he ran to her. "I don't want to be king anymore."

Sonya gave Julien a big bear hug.

"I was so hung up on who I was—who you was," Julien explained. "When all that really mattered was who we are *together*."

What Julien said struck Gia and Stefano. Julien was right—the circus was better when everyone was together. And "everyone" included Alex, Melman, Marty, and Gloria.

Kowalski walked up to Julien and plucked the dart out of his backside. "Skipper, it's titanium-tipped!" he said with a gasp.

"The crazy lady from Monte Carlo!" Skipper said, figuring it out.

Julien explained how Captain Dubois had snuck up on them. "She came out of the dead of the night, silent and deadly."

"The hippies got ambushed!" Skipper concluded.

A murmur arose from the circus animals.

Stefano spoke up. "We've got to help them!"

"*Nyet!*" Vitaly objected. "They are not circus. They are not our problem!"

This really angered Gia. "Are you going to

turn your back on them, like you did on us?" she asked Vitaly. "You used to care about more than just yourself. You had spirit. You had compassion. You were our hero. What happened to you? What happened to the old Vitaly?"

Vitaly was stunned to hear the truth. The only thing he could do was hang his head in shame. "The old Vitaly is no more," he admitted.

"That's Bolshevik!" Stefano shouted.

*Is it?* Vitaly thought. Was there a bit of the old Vitaly still inside?

Meanwhile, at the zoo, Alex heard people shouting. "Alex! Alex!" Slowly, he opened his eyes. Who was making all that noise?

Suddenly, his eyes snapped open fully. "Oh no!" Alex exclaimed. It was the crowd at the zoo!

"Alex? Where are you?" Marty asked groggily.

Melman stuck his head through the bars in the wall that separated him and Gloria and asked if she was okay.

"Ugh, what is happening?" Gloria asked as she lay dazed in her pool.

"Alex!" Marty shouted. He had just realized that they were back at the zoo.

"No, no, no! Wait, wait, wait!" Alex cried as he raced up from his pit and up to his pedestal. He looked through the bars of his enclosure and saw an enormous crowd chanting his name.

"Presenting the king of New York City, Alex the lion!" the mayor announced.

Alex leaped to the top of his rock and the adoring crowd cheered. And as fireworks lit up the sky, Alex looked back at his friends and they shared a look of disbelief and horror. Could it be? Were they really home?

"Alex! Alex!" the crowd shouted.

The answer to that question was definitely yes!

The mayor stood at a podium, surrounded by a crowd of New Yorkers. "Thank you. Thank you all for coming to this special celebration. And now, the woman who made this all possible, who brought Alex the lion and three other animals back to New York," the mayor announced. "And she's French!" he added. "Chantel Dubois."

"It's the crazy lady! She did this to us," Alex realized as Dubois walked up next to the mayor. The crowd cheered as the mayor handed her a big key and a gift bag.

"There's a restaurant guide and some almonds in there," the mayor said, pointing to the bag.

Then Dubois was presented with a big check.

"Merci, Monsieur Mayor. Merci, New York City," Dubois said. "I am both humbled and honored to receive your key and your gift bag. Your giant check, however, is an insult." And with that, she ripped it up!

The crowd gasped. Dubois took out a crumpled piece of paper from her pocket and unfolded it. Then she put on a pair of glasses and read, "When I was a little girl, Animal Control was considered a boy's club. But after I snapped the neck of my first hamster," she said, glancing up from her speech and smiling, "I knew this was my calling. So I accept this award not only on my own behalf, but on behalf of all the girls in the world who dare to dream of a world where the animals are dead."

The people in the crowd were stunned. What had she said? Dead animals? She *liked* when the animals were dead? But this was a zoo—a zoo with *live* animals. A man picked up his dog and held him tight, shielding his pet from this crazy lady.

"And this girl still dreams of dead animals," Dubois continued, "and a world *without* animals."

Dubois started to load her gun. As she continued to talk, she sounded crazier and crazier. "I want to make the phrase 'deer in the headlights' confusing and obsolete. And we can do it, if we do it together."

Hmm . . . that last part sounded familiar; it was just what Alex had said to the circus animals. But Alex's speech was a pep talk—something positive. This speech was downright creepy!

Slowly, the crowd started to back away. They wanted to escape from this crazy woman.

"Starting with one less lion," Dubois said as she pointed her gun at Alex.

Just then, music blared. Dubois looked at the crowd and saw they were staring toward the zoo gate. Then Gia swooped down and lifted Alex off the ground! Now they were both floating in the air.

"Gia! What are you doing here?" Alex asked as they swung onto the ledge of a building.

"I told you, Alex, if you do anything to harm this circus, you'll answer to me," Gia told him.

"Gia, I'm really sorry," Alex said.

"Don't apologize to me, apologize to them." Gia pointed down to the circus parade. They were marching right through the zoo. Balloons suspended the other animals.

"Look! A circus parade!" a kid in the crowd exclaimed as the elephants pushed the cannons through the zoo gates.

Stefano was locked and loaded in the cannon. "Fur power!" he shouted. Then *boom!* Stefano flew over Melman's and Gloria's enclosures, a rope in hand, and created a tightrope for Melman and Gloria to use as an escape.

"What are you standing there for, you fools?" Dubois shouted at her men. "Shoot them all!"

Gloria whistled to the dogs. The dogs, who were wearing their rocket-powered skates, climbed on the rope. *Whoosh!* The dogs shot up to Gloria, who grabbed them, juggled them like little balls, and shot them toward Dubois's men. The dogs then pummeled the men.

Meanwhile, the Penguins were hatching a plan of their own. They popped out of their pool and slid along their concrete island. Skipper kicked away a dish of fish bones, exposing a secret hole.

"Dive, dive, dive," Skipper ordered as the Penguins dived into the hole. The Penguins dropped down to a secret room. Quickly, Skipper pressed a button. A fish that hung on the wall opened its mouth and revealed a roller-coaster chair. The Penguins piled into the chair, pulled down the seat guard, and dropped down into a deep shaft. *Zoom!* The chair rocketed to the bottom, and the Penguins slipped out of the chair.

"Rico!" Skipper called.

Rico coughed up two keys, which the Penguins inserted into locks on a huge door.

"Execute!" Skipper ordered as the Penguins

turned the locks. "Since Y2K never happened, we might as well put it to good use," Skipper commented, referring to a big computer failure that never happened in the year 2000. The Penguins ran over to a giant penguin-shaped robot ship and climbed inside.

While the Penguins were belowground, the circus animals were trying to free the Zoosters aboveground.

One of Dubois's men shot a dart that narrowly missed Melman as Gloria lifted him onto the tightrope. The dart whizzed past Melman and crashed into a lamp. Shattered glass and electrical sparks flew everywhere. Some of the sparks landed in Marty's enclosure and ignited Marty's bed of straw.

"Whoa! Whoa!" Marty shouted as the flames shot up around his cage door.

"Marty!" Alex shouted as he watched Marty's cage go up in flames.

"Alex!" Marty panicked.

"Fire! Fire! Somebody help Marty!" Gloria shouted.

Alex tried to free Marty from his cage, but the flames were too hot.

Seeing Alex out in the open, Dubois thought she had a perfect shot. She ordered her men to shoot, but as soon as they raised their guns, an elephant swung down from a balloon and took them out.

"Stop and roll. Get me out of here! Somebody help!" Marty cried.

"Marty! Hang on!" Alex told him. "Just stay away from the flames."

Just then, Vitaly swung down from a balloon. His eyes focused on the flaming keyhole on the cage door. Then he growled, groomed his ears back, and ran toward the keyhole. *Poot!* Vitaly flew through the fiery keyhole, just like he had flown through the fiery hoop many years before.

"Suck in that gut," Vitaly told Marty as he grabbed hold of him.

Marty did what he was told and he and Vitaly flew though the keyhole together. Miraculously, they landed on the other side!

The crowd went wild. They thought this was part of the circus act!

Alex swung down from the balloons to greet them. "How did you do that?" he asked Vitaly. "That's impossible." Alex could not believe that Vitaly had gotten himself and Marty through that little keyhole. And the keyhole was on fire! And they came out unharmed!

"That's why the people love it," Vitaly told Alex. "Vitaly do the impossible!"

Just then, Gia called out to them. "Alex! To the balloons!"

As Alex headed to the balloons, Vitaly grabbed Stefano and put him inside a cannon. The cannon was raised up to the balloons.

The animals were making their escape, but it wouldn't be without a fight. Dubois was on her feet again. Her hair was a mess, and her lipstick was smudged, but her determination to destroy the animals was still strong.

"I've got your seal!" she called as she grabbed Stefano from inside the cannon.

Just then, the giant penguin-shaped robot ship rose out of the ground. Up, up it rose, until—*smash!*

It crashed through the top of the Reptile House and knocked Dubois out cold! Snakes slithered out of the house and into the Penguins' pool.

Marty couldn't believe what was going on, but Alex and Gia realized that their help had arrived. The penguin robot was their ticket out of there!

Alex saw the robot's jaws snap open and closed as its head spun around. Suddenly, he got an idea. "Marty, shoot me a line!" he shouted.

Marty jumped into his cannon.

"Frankie! Jonesy!" Alex called to the dogs. "You're with me!"

Alex lifted the dogs to his shoulders, and they jetted up to a floating platform just as Marty shot out of the cannon with a rope. He flew over the floating tightrope, past Melman and Gloria.

"A little help here!" Marty shouted. He had no idea how he was going to stop.

Just before Marty flew away, Melman and Gloria leaped off the high wire and grabbed the other end of Marty's rope. This helped slow down the flying Marty.

Then Alex flipped off the platform, Marty grabbed his wrists, and they swung toward Dubois. Alex knew they had to move fast because Dubois had Stefano cornered and was about to pull the trigger!

In the nick of time, Alex swooped in, grabbed Dubois and Stefano, and lifted them high into the air. Then he tossed Stefano to the floating platform, and the other animals caught him.

With Stefano safe, Alex had to figure out what to do with Dubois—whom he was still hanging on to! Dubois snarled at Alex. Alex shuddered—Dubois looked like an evil clown!

"Now, Marty!" Alex ordered. "Let go!"

Marty let go, and Alex and Dubois fell toward the pool of swimming cobras. The snakes snapped their jaws as they saw their dinner falling from the sky.

"Aquatic cobras!" Stefano said, watching the snakes.

Then, moments before becoming snake food, Alex shouted, "Light 'em up, fellas!"

Frankie and Jonesy (who were still on Alex) ignited their rocket skates, and pulled up at the last second.

"Jet pack!" Stefano exclaimed.

Alex and Dubois (powered by the dogs) flew toward the spinning penguin robot head. Alex waited until the robot's jaws opened and then he dropped Dubois. *Chomp!* Dubois was gobbled up! The crowd cheered.

"He's vanquished the evil clown!" Stefano cried.

Alex and the dogs spiraled up into a net that held hundreds of balloons. Reaching out with his claws, Alex sliced open the net, and the balloons fell to the children below.

Stefano, Vitaly, and Gia looked around in awe. Everything was happening just the way Alex had told them that day they took the Zoosters into the Circus Train—aquatic cobras, a jet pack, tossing balloons to children.

"Balloons to the children of the world! Trapeze Americano!" Stefano said through tears of joy.

"Yes, it's real," Vitaly admitted. The Zoosters really were circus!

Alex and the dogs landed safely on the floating circus rig.

"Good night, New York!" Alex said to the cheering crowd. "You've been a great crowd!"

"Ha-ha! Yes!" Vitaly agreed, giving Alex a high five. "You, my friend, are more circus than any circus that has ever circused in the circus!"

"Fur power," Alex said, raising his paw for a fist bump.

"Fur power," Vitaly agreed. Then he gave Alex a huge hug. Gia joined in, and then Stefano popped up. He wanted a hug, too!

The animals looked down from the floating platform and saw the penguin robot launch missiles into the air. The missiles exploded in the sky, giving the most amazing fireworks display that anyone had ever seen.

CHAPTER 20

Inside a Circus Train car, a zebra covered in polka dots and wearing a huge Afro wig sang a song: "Nuh, nuh, nuna, Afro circus!"

It was Marty, and his backup singers were the horses!

The Zoosters and the circus animals were happily riding the Circus Train as it chugged its way through the beautiful New England countryside.

"Hey, Skipper," Alex asked. "What did you end up doing with the crazy lady, anyway?"

Skipper chuckled. Dubois and her men were safe and sound inside shipping crates heading to—where else?—Madagascar!